Something else was bothering me.

Most of the cots here were occupied. And extra room was being prepared at St. Vincent's, Multnomah County, and Good Samaritan. I did a quick mental count. "We were told there were two hundred sick in the whole city," I said. How many patients were they expecting?

"There *were* two hundred," Hannah replied. "But that was yesterday. There are at least twice that now. And those are just the ones that have been reported."

I stopped in the center of the aisle. Two hundred yesterday, at least four hundred today. What did that mean for tomorrow? Or next week? And what about me? How long would it be before I ended up on one of those cots?

a
Death-
Struck
Year

MAKIIA LUCIER

HOUGHTON MIFFLIN HARCOURT
Boston   New York

www.hmhco.com

Text set in Garamond MT Std.

The Library of Congress has cataloged the hardcover edition as follows:
Lucier, Makiia.
A death-struck year / Makiia Lucier.
p. cm.
Summary: When the Spanish influenza epidemic reaches Portland,
Oregon, in 1918, seventeen-year-old Cleo leaves behind the
comfort of her boarding school to work for the Red Cross.
Includes bibliographical references.
1. Influenza epidemic, 1918–1919—Oregon—Portland—Juvenile fiction. [1. Influenza
epidemic, 1918–1919—Fiction. 2. Portland (Or.)—History—20th century—Fiction.] I. Title.
PZ7.L9715De 2014   [Fic]—dc23   2013037482

ISBN: 978-0-544-16450-5 hardcover
ISBN: 978-0-544-54118-4 paperback

Manufactured in the United States of America
DOC 10 9 8 7 6 5 4 3 2 1
4500562986

For Chris

PART ONE

And bound for the same bourn as I,
On every road I wandered by,
Trod beside me, close and dear,
The beautiful and death-struck year.
—A. E. Housman, *A Shropshire Lad*

CHAPTER ONE

Saturday, September 21, 1918

In the coming weeks, I would wish that I had done things differently. Thrown my arms around my brother, perhaps, and said, *I love you, Jack.* Words I hadn't spoken in years. Or held on a little tighter to Lucy and said, *Thank you. Thank you for watching over me, when my own mother could not.* But the distance between hindsight and foresight is as vast as the Pacific. And on my family's last evening in the city, my attention was fixed not on gratitude, certainly, but on myself. My sad, sorry, unambitious self.

Famous American Women: Vignettes from the Past and Present. Curled up on the settee, I read the book from first page to last, hoping inspiration would strike and put an end to my misery. *This!* This *is who you were meant to be, Cleo Berry. Go now and live your life.*

So far no luck.

I reviewed. Abigail Burgess Grant, lighthouse keeper at Matinicus Rock, Maine. I tried to picture it: the windswept coast, the salty air, the nearest neighbor miles away. *No,* I thought. *Too lonely.* I turned the page. Isabella Marie Boyd, wartime spy. *Too dangerous.* Geraldine Farrar, opera singer. *Not nearly enough talent.* I lingered over the entry for Eleanor Dumont, first female blackjack player, otherwise known as Madame Mustache. My spirits lifted a little as I imagined my brother's expression.

Lucy sat across from me, dressed for dinner and muttering over her itinerary. Jack stood near the parlor's window, pouring whiskey into a glass. His tie had been pulled loose, a navy suit jacket tossed onto the piano bench. We both favored our father, Jack and I, with gray eyes, hair black as pitch, and, to my sibling's everlasting embarrassment, dimples deep enough to launch a boat in. He glanced over, caught my eye, and tipped his glass in my direction. A friendly offer. Sixteen years my senior, my brother practiced an unorthodox form of guardianship: tolerant in some ways, overbearing in others. Whiskey was allowed. Young men were not.

I shook my head, then asked, "What does an ornithologist do?"

Jack placed the stopper into the decanter. "An ornithologist? Someone who studies birds, I believe."

Disappointed, I looked down. Florence Augusta Merriam Bailey, ornithologist. *No, too boring.* This was impossible.

4

"Do drink that behind a curtain, Jackson," Lucy said, looking out the window to where Mrs. Pike could be seen entering her home across the street. Mrs. Pike, the only neighbor we knew who took the Oregon Prohibition laws seriously. "That woman would have us sent to Australia if she could. Cleo as well."

"I don't think they ship criminals to Australia anymore, darlin'." But Jack obliged, moving out of sight.

Lucy frowned at me. "Are you sure you'll be all right while we're away?" She paused, careful not to look at her husband. "You do know you can always come with us."

Jack cleared his throat, not even attempting to mask a pained expression, and I couldn't help but smile. Tomorrow he and Lucy would be on a train to San Francisco to celebrate their thirteenth wedding anniversary. It was to be an extended vacation, with some business thrown in on Jack's part. They would be gone for six weeks.

"No one wants their sister around on an anniversary trip," I said. "It's the opposite of romantic."

"Thank you, Cleo," Jack said. Lucy looked ready to argue.

"I'll be fine. Truly," I added, knowing the real reason she worried. "We're too far west for the influenza. Everyone has said so."

I had heard of the Spanish influenza. Who had not? A particularly fierce strain of flu, it had made its way down the eastern seaboard, sending entire families to the hospitals, crippling the military training bases. The newspapers were filled with gruesome tales from Boston, Philadelphia, and New York. Cities so far away, they could have been part of another country. But that was the extent of it. We were safe here in Oregon. In Portland. The Spanish flu had no interest in the northwestern states.

"Very well," Lucy said, defeated. "But here, this is for you." She handed me her itinerary. I looked it over. It contained their train arrival and departure information, as well as the names of friends located the entire length of the Pacific coast whom I could call on for assistance should I need it. Also, a reminder that they would be returning on November third, a Sunday, and would stop directly at St. Helen's Hall to bring me home.

The same old complaint lodged on the tip of my tongue, and I bit down, hard. I didn't want to spoil their last evening by showing how unhappy I was. They knew already. But inside, I wanted to kick something.

Many of my schoolmates had homes outside the city, traveling in from towns such as Coos Bay, Eugene, Bend, and Sisters. Others hailed from farther out: Juneau, Coeur d'Alene, Walla Walla, even Honolulu. Some lived in the student dormitories during the week and spent weekends with their families. Others traveled home only during the holidays.

I was a day student. Jack drove me to school each morning on the way to his office, and I walked home in the afternoon. Or rode the streetcar. But while Jack and Lucy were away, the house was to be closed up. Our housekeeper, Mrs. Foster, given leave. She would also be traveling tomorrow, by steamboat, to visit her son in Hood River.

I had begged to be allowed to remain at home on my own, not liking one bit the thought of six weeks in the dormitories — away from my comfortable bedroom, away from any hope of privacy. My brother was unsympathetic. He had boarded throughout his own school years. He said it built character. And that I shouldn't grumble, because no matter how awful a girls' dormitory might be, a boys' residence was a thousand times worse.

I skimmed the rest of Lucy's notes. I was to telephone the Fairmont San Francisco once a week, each Saturday, to confirm I remained in the land of the living. *Good grief,* I thought.

"Good Lord," Jack said at the same time, peering over my shoulder. "Lucy, she's seventeen, not seven."

Lucy gave him a look, then proceeded to guide me through every part of their schedule. I resisted the urge to close my eyes. The smell of roasting potatoes drifted from the kitchen, and I remembered Mrs. Foster was preparing a salmon for our last supper. Beyond Lucy, the luggage was piled high in the front hall, enough trunks and suitcases and hatboxes to send six people off in style.

Trying to be discreet, I lifted a corner of the itinerary and peeked at my book. Maria Mitchell, first American woman astronomer, director of the observatory at Vassar College. Kate Furbish, botanical artist. Harriet Boyd Hawes, pioneering archaeologist. My head fell back against the cushions, and I sighed, long and tortured.

"Who has let in the bear?" Lucy exclaimed.

I straightened. While I'd been woolgathering, Jack had settled beside Lucy, his glass cradled in one hand, his other arm flung across the back of the settee. Two pairs of eyes regarded me with amused exasperation.

"All this heavy breathing," Lucy continued. "*What* is troubling you, Cleo?"

Well, what harm could come from telling them? They might be able to help.

"It's only September," Lucy said, after I explained my dilemma. "There are nine months left of school."

"You can't be the only one trying to figure things out," Jack added. "I wouldn't feel like a chump just yet."

"But I do. I *do* feel like a chump." I counted my friends on my hand. "Louisa is getting married in July." I ticked off one finger. "Her fiancé is almost thirty and has already lost most of his hair. But he's very rich, and her papa thinks he's very handsome."

Jack snorted. Lucy laughed, smoothing the skirt of her sapphire-blue dress. My sister-in-law was small and fair-haired and pretty, with eyes more amber than brown. No one was ever surprised to learn she had been born in Paris. She *looked* French and carried herself in a way that made me feel like a baby giraffe in comparison. Tall and gangling, with Mrs. Foster constantly having to let out my skirt hems.

A second finger ticked off. "Fanny is moving to New York to study poetry. She plans to become a bohemian and smoke cigarettes." Recalling this bit of information, I felt a twinge of envy. New York City. Tea at the Plaza. All those museums. How glamorous it sounded.

Jack interrupted my thoughts. "What kind of unorthodox institution are those women running?"

I dropped my hand. "Rebecca already has her early acceptance letter from Barnard. Myra is sending in her application to the University of Washington. Charlotte, Emmaline, and Grace are all going to the University of Oregon." I set the book and the itinerary on the table, beside a well-thumbed copy of *American Architect*. "And Margaret will wait for Harris. Then there's me. I *do* know I want to attend university. Maybe study art. But I don't really care to paint portraits. Or landscapes." I bit my lip, considering. "Maybe I can study French. But what does one do after studying French?"

"Marry," Jack said. Lucy smacked his knee lightly, but she smiled.

I looked into the fire, feeling gloomy. My schoolmates at least had an inkling of a plan. I had nothing. No plan. No dream. No calling. The uncertainty bothered me, like a speck in the eye that refused to budge.

"I am utterly without ambition," I said.

At this, Jack leaned forward, pointing his glass at me. "Now you're just being melodramatic. Not everyone leaves school knowing their life's purpose, Cleo. And those who do often change their minds ten times over." He waved a hand toward the window. "Sometimes you need to go out in the world and live a little first."

Lucy reached over, gathered the itinerary, and tapped it against the table until the edges lined up. "Go to university," she said, sympathetic. "See what interests you. Young ladies today have the freedom to do what they like."

"*Except* become a bohemian," Jack said with a warning glance. He tossed back the rest of his drink and stood. "There are enough sapphists in this city as it is."

CHAPTER TWO

Wednesday, September 25, 1918

Aut viam inveniam aut . . . aut facile?"

"No! It's *faciam,* Cleo. Not *facile.* 'I will either find a way or make one.' We've gone over this before," Grace said.

It was nine o'clock at night. I was in my dormitory room, lying on a rickety old bed that had been moved from the attic for my temporary stay. Grace sat cross-legged on her quilt, her Latin textbook open before her. Across from us, Fanny lounged against a pile of pillows, reading poetry. Something depressing like Byron, likely, because she never read anything but. In the fourth bed, beside Fanny, Margaret wrote a letter to Harris and ignored us all.

"Memorizing Latin is just like memorizing French or Italian, and you know both," Grace continued. "You're making this more difficult than it needs to be."

"I'm not!" I said, feeling stupid. "And why should we learn

it? Who uses Latin anymore? Old men, that's who. It's a dead language."

"Well, you're the one who's going to be dead if you don't pass this class," Grace said.

Fanny smirked. Like the rest of us, she wore a white nightgown that reached her ankles. But Fanny's was topped with a blue satin wrapper covered in tiny silver stars. There would be hell to pay if Miss Elliot, our headmistress, happened by. Blue satin did not fall under the school's approved category of sensible white cotton night clothing.

"Grace is right, Cleo," Fanny said. *"Diligentia maximum etiam mediocris ingeni subsidium."*

Margaret glanced up from her letter. "Oh, do shut up, Fanny!" she snapped. Fanny's smile evaporated.

I sat up. "What? What did she say?"

"Nothing." Grace cast her own withering look in Fanny's direction. "Ignore her. Just listen for the roots. It's easy. *Fortiter in re, suaviter in modo.*" She flicked a blond braid over one shoulder, so long the ends skimmed the pages of her textbook.

A month ago, my own hair had been just as lengthy. But Lucy had decided to have hers shaped into a bob. I'd taken one look at the result, thrown caution to the wind, and cut my hair off too. Miss Elliot huffed and puffed whenever she saw me, saying it was a completely inappropriate hairstyle for a young lady. Lucy had only laughed and said it was impossible to please everyone.

I tried to concentrate. It was difficult. Next door Emmaline practiced her violin. Schubert's *L'Abeille,* a piece that always made me feel as though I were trapped in a beehive. Aggravated, I reached up and pounded on the wall with the side of my fist. The buzzing stopped but only for a moment. Emmaline started up again, and I wished I were back on King Street. In my nice quiet home. As I had wished every day this week.

"Cleo!" Grace said, exasperated. *"Fortiter in re, suaviter in modo."*

I concentrated. *Fort* was the French word for *powerful. Modo* was Italian for *manner. In,* thankfully, meant *in.* But what about *re* and *suaviter?* Powerful in blank, blank in manner. The faintest memory stirred, and I tried, "'Resolute in action, gentle in manner'?"

"Good! See? *Qui tacet consentire videtur?"*

"'He who is tacit'. . .'" I began. Grace's expression darkened. "Um, 'He who is silent gives consent'?"

"Yes!"

I jumped as a crash sounded from another room, followed by girls giggling like lunatics. No one in our room batted an eye, though. They'd had years to get used to living in a zoo. I drew my knees up and wrapped both arms around them.

If I were at home, toothpowder wouldn't clog the sinks, and clumps of hair wouldn't stop the drains. The halls would smell like lemons, the way Mrs. Foster preferred. Not like damp stockings. Or feet. Or the hard-boiled eggs Fanny snuck in from dinner.

Grace turned a page. *"Si post fata venit gloria non propero."*

"I know that one," I said. "'If one must die to be recognized, I can wait.'"

Fanny rose and wandered out of the room. In her blue wrap and with her brown hair loose and flowing, I grudgingly admitted she would make a very good bohemian in New York City.

"The door!" Margaret called.

Fanny disappeared, leaving it wide open. I scowled after her as well, having just deciphered her earlier insult. *Diligentia maximum etiam mediocris ingeni subsidium.* "Diligence is a very great help even to a mediocre intelligence." Trollop. Just once, it would be nice to think of a retort at the exact right moment. Not five minutes later, when the effect was lost completely.

"*Dulce bellum inexpertis,*" Grace droned.

I sighed. "'War is sweet to those who never fought'?"

"*Faber est quisque fortunae suae.*"

"'Every man is the architect of his own fortune.'"

Through the open doorway, I glimpsed red.

"*Amare et —*"

"Louisa!" I yelled. When there was no response from the hall, I jumped off the bed and was out the door in an instant.

"Louisa."

Louisa turned. There was no mistaking the guilt in her brown eyes. "Yes?"

"Yes? Is that all you're going to say?" Louisa had yet to change into her nightgown. I looked pointedly at the cherry-red sweater she wore over her white blouse. My cherry-red sweater. "One usually asks to borrow clothing *before* wearing it."

"I'm sorry. But I couldn't find you and . . ." She smiled sweetly, not fooling me one bit. "May I borrow your sweater, Cleo?"

"No." I held out a hand.

"Well." Louisa pouted and sulked. She removed the sweater and dropped it into my hand, before marching down the hall to her own room. A door slammed.

If I were at home, no one would enter my bedroom without permission. Lucy wouldn't steal my clothing. Or my shampoo, which had also mysteriously gone missing.

"How do you bear it?" I asked no one in particular.

Fanny brushed by me on her way back into the room. "My mother says there's a history of kleptomania in that family. I told you to keep the door locked."

Emmaline was playing a new piece, one I did not recognize. I stood in my doorway, listening as the music reached a violent, off-key crescendo. I inspected my sweater. A button was missing.

Jack and Lucy wouldn't be home until the third of November.

Five and a half more weeks.

CHAPTER THREE

Monday, September 30, 1918

Greta lay sprawled and lifeless with her head against my skirt. The rag doll was four feet tall, the same height as its owner, with red yarn hair. Her blue gingham dress looked as if it had been pulled through a dirt field. She was missing both eyes.

Baffled, I studied the doll, then looked at the six-year-old playing at my feet. "What happened, Emily?" I asked. "Did you pluck her eyes out?"

"Anna did it," Emily said. "She told me Greta's button eyes gave her the willies. She pulled them out while I was having my bath."

"Lord," I said under my breath.

Emily's brown eyes were big and anxious. "You'll fix her, won't you, Cleo?"

"I'll fix her. Don't worry."

We were in the stairway that led from the dormitories to the main floor. I perched on a step halfway down. Just below, on the small landing, Emily played with an elaborate set of paper dolls. Murky oil landscapes lined the walls above us, each painting framed in blackened wood. It was just after four in the afternoon, and most of the other girls were off finishing their schoolwork or outside. Emily and I had the stairway to ourselves.

"Does Greta give you the willies?" Emily asked.

She certainly did. Emily dragged her everywhere she could, and it always felt like the doll's black button eyes watched my every move. Poor Anna. I would be tempted to yank Greta's eyes out too, if I had to share a room with her.

"Greta's a perfectly lovely doll," I said. "I'll talk to Anna and make sure she takes more care with your toys."

Cheered, Emily returned her attention to the paper dolls. Her brown hair was set in two braids that looped the sides of her head like earmuffs. Emily's roommate, Anna, was also six. The girls were among the school's youngest boarders. Anna's family lived in Tigard, just outside Portland. She spent weekends at home. Emily's family was from Honolulu. She sailed back to the island once a year, in the summer.

I rifled through my school satchel for a small sewing kit, then set one of Greta's button eyes back in place. The grime had been rinsed off, and the black button, two inches round, was nice and shiny.

"Cleo?"

"Hmm?" I hunched over Greta. The light in the stairway was poor, and I wondered if I should fix the doll back in my room near a window. I dismissed the thought. Fanny was there, more snappish than usual. All things considered, I preferred the dim staircase. When there was no response from Emily, I glanced up. The child looked back at me, uncertain.

"Did Anna do something else?" I asked, pulling the needle taut.

Emily shook her head. "No, but I forgot Greta in the library this morning. I went back for her, and I heard Mr. Brownmiller and Miss Abernathy talking . . ."

I paused. "What did you hear?"

"Well, Mr. Brownmiller said that people in Phil . . . Phila . . ."

"Philadelphia," I prompted.

"He said that people in Philadelphia were dropping like flies. Because of the Spanish influenza. He said they're running out of coffins. Is that true, Cleo? And what about us? Are we going to drop dead too?" Emily's voice quivered.

I bit back a sigh. Mr. Brownmiller had been the school librarian for as long as I could remember. Miss Abernathy taught upper school history. I thought they should know better than to say such things in a school full of girls. Most of us had light feet. We lurked in every corner, just waiting to hear something we shouldn't. Like the time Margaret overheard Miss Elliot say that Miss Kovich, our nurse, had been let go because she'd had an affair with a married man and was in a family way. Or the time Fanny heard Miss Bishop sobbing all over Mrs. Brody in the kitchen because her sweetheart had married someone else. There were no secrets at St. Helen's Hall. Not one.

I set Greta aside — the needle poking out of her eye — and wondered what to say. For I'd heard the same shocking stories about Philadelphia and the rest of the East Coast. And then some.

Fanny's sister had told her about a fine young family man in Boston who had fallen ill and become delirious. A nurse was sent to his home. But when she left his room, just for a moment, he pulled a revolver from the bureau drawer and shot himself dead.

Emmaline's cousin had read about a man in New York who went to help his neighbor, the undertaker, transport bodies to a warehouse once the morgue grew overcrowded. He saw the body of a friend, with whom he had chatted the day before. He also stumbled across the girl who helped his wife around the house.

There was a shortage of coffins in Philadelphia. They were burying people in mass graves with only the clothes on their backs. Louisa's sister had heard of a family who lost a seven-year-old boy. They were so desperate to have him buried in something, *anything,* that they placed him in a twenty-pound macaroni box. A little boy. Buried in a pasta box.

I thought about these stories. Dreadful stories. And for the thousandth time, I was grateful that the entire width of the country lay between such awfulness and my home.

"The Spanish influenza *is* very bad in Philadelphia," I finally said. "But do you know what?"

"What?"

"Philadelphia is thousands of miles away. Which means the influenza is thousands of miles away. I can show you."

Emily cocked her head. "How?"

"On a map. I'll finish with Greta, and we'll go down to the library. Then you can see that the flu is too far away to hurt anyone here. How does that sound?"

Emily was quiet for a minute. Then her expression cleared and she agreed, returning her attention to the paper dolls. She danced them around on the landing and sang:

> *"Dear Pig, are you willing to sell for one shilling*
> *Your ring?" Said the Piggy, "I will."*
> *So they took it away, and were married next day*
> *By the Turkey who lives on the hill.*

I went back to work on Greta, knowing I would have "The Owl and the Pussycat" stuck in my head for the rest of the day. After finishing off the first eye, I reached for the scissors and snipped the excess string. The button wobbled, but it would hold for the time being. Still, I mentally crossed *seamstress* off my list of future occupations.

After the second button was sewn on and a small tear in Greta's dress mended, Emily and I gathered our belongings and trooped hand in hand to the school library. Mr. Brownmiller's globe, along with the city of Philadelphia, held Emily's attention for all of ten seconds before she looked out a window and spotted her friends playing tag on the front lawn. She dashed outside and joined Anna, who was apparently forgiven for Greta's earlier disfigurement. I followed, the doll tucked beneath an arm.

St. Helen's Hall was a grand old building: red brick covered in ivy, with a bell tower, a curved double staircase leading to the main doors, and a second tower room that Miss Elliot used as an office. Dozens of students dotted the lawn, taking advantage of the brisk but pleasant afternoon. It was nearly October. We all knew our mild days were numbered.

I settled onto an empty bench beneath an oak tree. The doll flopped beside me. I took my sketchbook from my satchel and fanned the pages until I found one near the back that was fresh and new. My pencil tapped against my leg for a minute or two while I studied everything around me. I sketched the building, shading in the trees and the ivy, trying to capture the sunlight glancing off the windows. I added students to the lawn, posing Emily in a somersault with her legs kicked up in the air, underthings exposed, as she'd just been. I drew Miss Elliot, broom-thin and dressed in black, her snow-white hair piled high. She scolded Charlotte for riding her bicycle on the grass. Just as I finished with Margaret sitting on the front steps, scribbling madly on paper, I heard someone running toward me. I looked up and saw Grace.

"There you are!" She pushed Greta aside and collapsed onto the bench. Her face was flushed and her spectacles crooked. She looked like she'd run around the entire school twice.

"What's wrong?" I asked, alarmed.

Grace caught her breath, and then spoke in a great rush. "I was walking by Miss Gillette's classroom. She was talking to Miss Abernathy, and I heard her say that soldiers arrived at Camp Lewis a few days ago. Their train came from somewhere back east. Boston, I think." Emily and Anna fell in a giggling heap nearby. Grace lowered her voice. "The soldiers—they're all sick, Cleo. Every last one of them. They're saying it's Spanish influenza."

A tight, unpleasant feeling gathered inside me. "It could just be regular old influenza," I argued. "It's almost October. How do they know for sure?"

Grace looked frightened. "Miss Gillette says it's not like any influenza they've ever seen. And two of the men have died already. Died, Cleo! You don't just *die* after two days of the flu!"

I gripped my pencil. My mouth felt, suddenly, as if it were filled with ashes.

"Cleo." Grace wrung her hands. "Oh, Cleo. Camp Lewis."

I stared at Greta. She looked up at me with her two button eyes. It struck me that I would have no comforting words to offer Emily now. Because Camp Lewis wasn't thousands of miles away, in some godforsaken part of the country. No. Camp Lewis was an easy train ride north. In Washington.

Only one state away.

I sidled around a corner, quick as a cat. Past the music room, the art studio, the science laboratory, the library. I crept by the teachers' parlor, where muffled conversation rose and fell behind thick doors. Dinner was long over; the halls were empty. Thankfully. It would not do to be seen wandering about at this hour. I should have been in my room, finishing my homework and preparing for bed.

Not helping a friend with a ghastly, *ghastly* task.

At the end of the hall, I slipped into the dining room. Moonlight filtered through the diamond-cross windows, casting shadows onto long, wooden tables. Usually, the chatter of one hundred and fifty girls filled the space, along with the clink of silverware and the scraping of chairs against the floor. Tonight the silence swallowed me up. I made my way to the far end of the room, where the teachers' table stood upon a slightly raised dais, and opened the door.

Margaret stood in the center of a sizable kitchen, swimming

in one of Mrs. Brody's aprons. She jumped at my entrance, her blue eyes wide. A scrub brush clattered onto the countertop.

"It's just me," I said, apologetically. I walked into the room, careful not to trip over the apple crates scattered across the tiles. I could guess the menu for the week: baked apples, apple dumplings, apple stuffing, apple cider, applesauce. With the food shortages and inflation caused by the war, Mrs. Brody, the school cook, had grown especially careful. We would be eating apples every day until the last one was gone.

Margaret pressed a hand to her chest, leaving a damp imprint on the white cloth. "Honestly, Cleo," she said, glowering. "I thought you were Lizzie Borden."

Two metal buckets had been placed on the counter before her. I peeked in one of them, recoiling when I saw it was filled with discarded nectarine pits, chunks of slimy fruit still hanging from most of them.

"Ugh," I said. "How much longer?"

Margaret made a face. "Ten days."

"What rotten luck."

Last weekend Mrs. Brody had caught Margaret trying to sneak in through the kitchen well past curfew. Her hair was mussed and her blouse misbuttoned, though she refused to tell anyone where she had gone. Or whom she had met. It was not hard to guess. Her parents were away, so Margaret's true day of reckoning was postponed. In the meantime, she was to collect the fruit pits from our plates and scrub them clean before they were delivered to the Red Cross.

The pits were needed for carbon. The carbon was needed for gas masks.

I watched as Margaret scooped a pit from one bucket, scrubbed the flesh free with her brush, and tossed it into the second container. I glanced around. Another, equally enormous apron hung from a hook beside one of the iceboxes. I put it on, wrapping the belt three times around my waist before securing it behind me. I slid onto a stool and reached into the first bucket. Saliva and old fruit coated my fingers. *Ghastly.* Swallowing hard, I fumbled with the slippery pit, scrubbed the offending flesh off, and tossed it into the second bucket. It was trickier than it looked, and a thousand times more disgusting.

Margaret watched my struggle. A small grateful smile replaced her frown. "Thanks, Cleo."

"Humph," I replied, though her smile made up for it a little. Margaret rarely smiled these days. It was more common to see her sitting at her desk, staring off into space, twisting the gold locket Harris had given her for her birthday. I couldn't remember the last time I'd seen her look anything other than miserable.

I held my hand over the trash bin. Fruit slithered from my fingers into the receptacle. "Grace told me about Harris," I said. "I'm sorry, Meg."

Margaret's eyes flickered to mine, then dropped. "His mother had a fit when she heard." There was a slight catch to her voice. "Harry says she won't leave her room, not even to eat."

I reached over and squeezed Margaret's fruit-coated hand, near tears myself. Last year, only months after we'd entered the war, a draft had been passed, requiring the enlistment of all able-bodied men aged twenty-one to thirty. Harris was nineteen. But recently, the draft had been extended to those aged eighteen to forty-five. The first to be called up were young men without wives or dependents. Grace's brother, Peter, had already left the University of Oregon for training. So had Fanny's brothers, James and Robert. They were boys we knew. Brothers and chums. I thought of Margaret's good-natured Harris Brown. And sweethearts.

My stomach knotted again, but this time it had nothing to do with pits. My own brother was thirty-four years old.

"Will he have time to come home?" I released her hand. "Or will he leave straight from school?"

"He'll take the train home next week." Margaret sniffled, then dashed away a tear with her sleeve. "He can stay a few days."

"Where will he go? Not Camp Lewis?"

Margaret shook her head. "Fort Stevens," she said, naming the military base at the mouth of the Columbia River. "Harry thinks there'll be an official quarantine announcement at Camp Lewis soon. Only doctors and nurses are being allowed through the gates." She gave up on the pits, staring down at her reddened hands. "At least he'll be close by. Some of his schoolmates are being sent to California."

"Maybe he won't have to leave Oregon at all." I tried to sound reassuring. "The newspapers are saying it won't last much longer. I heard it could all be over by Thanksgiving."

"You don't believe that, do you?" Bitterness crept into Margaret's tone. "How long have they been saying that? 'The war will be over by Thanksgiving. Our boys will be home by Christmas.'" She flung a pit into the bucket so hard it *thwang*ed against the metal side. "The newspapers say lots of things, Cleo."

Stung, I said nothing. The silence stretched on for a time, broken only by the sound of pits hitting metal. I glanced at Margaret. A question hovered on the tip of my tongue. I hesitated, because I knew saying the words aloud would only make them harder to ignore.

"Camp Lewis isn't very far." I wiped my hands on Mrs. Brody's apron. "Do you think we'll see it here?"

Margaret didn't answer at first. "My father says we won't," she finally said. "He says the influenza never lasts this long. That it's bound to run its course before it reaches Portland." She lifted a handful of pits and studied them, though I had the feeling she saw something else entirely. "I think they try to pretend that we're still children. That we won't figure it out for ourselves." She opened her hand, allowing the pits to slide back into the bucket. She looked at me across the countertop, her blue eyes dark and sober. "But it's everywhere else, Cleo. Why not here?"

It was midnight. The witching hour. I lay sleepless, listening as Grace's snores filled the room. My mind whirled. I thought about the soldiers at Camp Lewis. About coffin shortages. About Jack and Lucy, hundreds of miles away in San Francisco. I tossed and turned, pounding my pillow into a shapeless lump. Finally, I gave up.

Carefully, so as not to wake anyone, I reached for my wrapper. I slipped out of the room and crept down the hall in bare feet. A single table lamp provided the only source of light. I gripped the banister and descended the staircase, wincing as the old steps creaked beneath me.

The library was located on the main floor just beyond the staircase. I felt my way about in near darkness for the door. Mr. Brownmiller never locked the room. I switched on a lamp, illuminating mahogany shelves that rose from floor to ceiling. Study tables were scattered about, along with wing-backed chairs the color of rubies. Mr. Brownmiller's giant globe stood beside his desk. The library smelled faintly of lemons, reminding me, though I wished it didn't, of home.

I wandered over to the closest shelf, one finger trailing along the spines as I searched for something to bore me into unconsciousness. *Meditations, The Muse in Arms, Ethan Frome.* Just as I was about to tug *Richard III* free, another title caught my eye. I reached down and pulled *Aesop's Fables* from a low shelf.

I settled into a chair, reaching behind me to switch on a second lamp. The book was oversize, with a deep purple cover bordered in gold ivy. I had been six years old the first time I'd seen this copy. That morning the sun poured in through the classroom windows, so bright I could see the dust motes suspended in the air. I'd been scribbling on my slate, practicing my penmanship with the rest of the girls in the lower school, while Miss Gillette wrote out the day's lesson on the chalkboard. And then I had started to cry. It happened sometimes, tears that would come from nowhere. One moment I felt fine, and the next I would remember what I'd lost with a keenness that left me breathless.

The whole class had ground to a halt, shocked. There was a giggle from Fanny, quickly shushed. Miss Gillette escorted me to Miss Elliot's office, murmuring words such as *There, there* and *You poor dear.*

Jack was summoned to take me home for the day. I was sent to wait for him in the library with Mr. Brownmiller. I sat on the floor in a puddle of white muslin. A book on horses lay unopened before me. An hour passed. There was no one else about, Mr. Brownmiller having gone off to run a brief errand. Once again, my tears fell unchecked. Pushing the book aside, I wrapped my arms around my legs and buried my face in my knees.

It was not long before I realized I was not alone. I lifted my head. Jack stood several feet away, hands buried in the pockets of a tan suit. He perused the bookshelf, seemingly unaware of my presence. I glanced around, wondering if I had somehow become invisible.

Finally, he glanced down. "Do you know the stories of Aesop?" he asked, making no mention of my tears.

I shook my head, sniffling, and stared at the rug. I did not know what to make of this brother, whom I did not remember but who looked so much like my papa it hurt to watch him. Jack had gone to an important school in Paris, I knew, where they taught you to build beautiful buildings. Mama had said Jack and Lucy were to stay in France, and we would visit them the following spring. But that was before. Jack had come home, appearing at the Keatings', where I had gone to stay after the accident. My brother was kind. But I knew he was only here because he had to be. Because of me.

"No?" Jack selected a large purple book from the shelf. With little regard for his suit, he dropped to the rug beside me and crossed his legs. He set the book aside before reaching over, lifting me beneath my arms, and plopping me in front of him. Jack settled *Aesop's Fables* onto my lap and paged through it.

"When I was your age," his voice rumbled against my back, "I always liked 'The Tortoise and the Hare' and 'The Goose That Laid the Golden Eggs.' But my favorite was . . . ah. Here it is. Would you like me to read it to you?"

"Yes." I studied the title. "Grief and His Due." Below it was a picture of a bearded man dressed in a flowing robe. He sat on a throne, one hand stretched toward the dark-haired woman who knelt before him. The woman's head was bowed, and tears poured from her eyes to form a small lake on the ground before her. I swiped at my damp cheek, hesitant.

Jack cleared his throat. "'Grief and His Due. When the Roman god Jupiter was assigning the various lesser gods their privileges, it so happened that Grief was not present with the rest. But when all had received their share, Grief arrived and claimed his due. Jupiter was at a loss, for there was nothing left for Grief. At last, Jupiter decided that Grief should be given the tears that are shed for the dead. Thus it is the same with Grief as it is with the other gods. The more you honor him, the more lavish he is with his gifts. It is not well, therefore, to mourn long for loved ones. Else Grief, whose sole pleasure is in such mourning, will be quick to send fresh cause for tears.'"

Jack tipped my chin and studied me, his gray eyes somber. "Do you know what this story is trying to tell us, Cleo?"

I was unsure. "That . . . that I should try not to be so sad all the time?"

A small smile appeared on his face. "You can be sad. I miss them too." He wiped my tears away with his thumb. "But sometimes the hardest decision is choosing to be happy again."

My lip wobbled. Four months had passed since Mama and Papa's carriage had careened off the road into the ravine. Four months since I had gone to bed without having to cry myself to sleep.

For a long time, the only sound came from the *ticktock*ing of the grandfather clock in the hall. My brother, this stranger, pressed a kiss to the top of my head. He drew out his pocket watch — Papa's old watch — and flipped it open. "Well, it's nearly time for lunch," he said. "And I have a hankering for Swetland's. What do you say?"

"Truly?" I asked. Swetland's was an ice cream parlor. And a candy shop.

Jack smiled. "Don't tell Lucy."

The memory calmed me. I read through the old stories — "The Lion and the Ass," "The Mice and the Weasels," "The Monkey as King" — until my eyelids drooped. Placing the book on a small table, I pulled my wrapper tight around me. Only then was I able to sleep.

CHAPTER FOUR

Friday, October 11, 1918

As one of the most influential philosophers of the Enlightenment Age, Immanuel Kant believed in a life lived autonomously." Miss Abernathy wrote on the chalkboard as she spoke, underscoring Kant's name with a flourish. She dropped the chalk and faced the class. "His motto was the phrase *'Sapere aude!,'* which translates to . . ."

I propped my chin on my hand and looked out the window, where a heavy rainfall obliterated the view. Some cities had proper seasons: spring, summer, winter, fall. But here in Portland, we just had wet and wetter. And sometimes, during the summer, slightly less wet. Rain was a constant in our town; today was no exception. Most of the time I didn't mind it, but this morning it just made me feel dreary. I listened to Miss Abernathy go on and on about long-dead German philosophers and felt my eyelids droop. I blinked slowly, once, twice . . .

"If you would be so kind as to read the passage on Kant, Miss Berry."

I jolted. A pencil sailed off my desk and across the aisle, landing by Grace's shoe. Miss Abernathy looked at me, brows arched, missing nothing. "Page fourteen."

"Yes, ma'am." I cleared my throat. Grace offered a sympathetic glance. She set the pencil on my desk.

I looked at my open textbook and started: "'What is Enlightenment? Enlightenment is the triumph of the human being over his self-imposed immaturity. It demands nothing more than freedom—the freedom that consists in making public use, under all circumstances, of one's reason. For it is the birthright of every human being to think for himself.'"

"Thank you, Miss Ber—" Miss Abernathy began, but a sharp knock on the door interrupted her.

Miss Bishop, the headmistress's secretary, stood in the doorway, her pretty face harried. Beside her was a man I didn't recognize. He was portly, with a thick broom mustache. He clutched a briefcase.

Frowning, Miss Abernathy met her visitors in the doorway. The three engaged in feverish whispers. The man reached into his briefcase and handed Miss Abernathy a single sheet of paper.

"Today?" I heard my teacher ask. The man threw his hands up in a hopeless-looking gesture.

I glanced around at my schoolmates, all dressed in identical uniforms: short navy jackets, long navy skirts, crisp white blouses. They looked as nervous as I felt. We fidgeted in our seats. Only Margaret sat perfectly still. She occupied a desk in the back row, her spine as straight as one of Jack's drafting rulers, her gaze fastened on the trio by the door.

I watched my friend, remembering our conversation in the kitchen. After the soldiers had fallen ill at Camp Lewis, the influenza had made front-page news in the *Oregonian*. As a precaution, the city health office ordered theater managers to evict anyone who coughed and sneezed from the premises or face legal action. An announcement in yesterday's edition had gone one step further. As of today, all soldiers and sailors were banned from Portland theaters.

Here at St. Helen's, the teachers smiled less and whispered more. Everywhere you looked, students huddled over newspapers. Even the younger girls. A single sneeze was met with a wary glance and a quick backwards step. Two sneezes earned one a trip to the infirmary. Miss Elliot insisted there was no need to panic. These were simply precautionary measures.

Lucy and Jack had telephoned. I could hear the worry in their voices when they suggested canceling their trip and returning home. I wanted to agree. But I knew I would have felt guilty forever. So I said, *Stay. There is no influenza in Portland. Not one case. I'll be fine.* And after a lengthy conversation with Miss Elliot, they decided to stay.

Just thinking about the last week brought on a nervous, persistent headache and an uneasy feeling in my stomach. I tried to ignore it. I tried very hard to believe we were still safe here.

I turned back in my seat just in time to see the man leave. Miss Bishop's skirt swished around the door frame as she followed, the rapid *click-click-click* of her shoes echoing down the hall.

Miss Abernathy held a single sheet of paper in her hand. Her expression was troubled, though her voice was as calm as always. "Ladies, I have an important announcement to make." She glanced down at the paper. "'As a precautionary measure and effective immediately, the Portland Health Department is closing all schools, public and private, within the city limits.'"

A collective gasp filled the room, followed by the sound of a dozen girls attempting to speak over one another. My arm shot straight into the air and was lost in a sea of frantic waving hands. Closing the schools? Today? I don't know what I had expected, but it was not this.

Miss Abernathy held up a palm to silence the onslaught. "Let me finish, please. I promise I will answer your questions as best I can once I'm through."

Arms dropped. As I waited for Miss Abernathy to continue,

dread snaked its way down the back of my neck. Because some-thing smelled off. *A precautionary measure,* she had said. We already practiced precautionary measures. We washed our hands, left the windows open during the day, sent anyone who looked suspicious to the infirmary. But shutting down the entire school system? That sounded like far more than a precaution.

Miss Abernathy returned her attention to the notice. "'Thirty-six thousand students and one thousand teachers will be affected by this order. In addition, all public gatherings have been banned. There will be no theater performances, club activities, parades, pool halls, or church services.'"

"No church!"

"No theaters!"

"Cleo!" Grace hissed beside me. I ignored her, trying to absorb one shock after another. Public gatherings. What about the train stations? My brother and Lucy would leave San Francisco as soon as they heard. I was certain they would. Would they be able to travel by train? Fear clutched me as another thought struck.

How safe were the trains?

For the second time, Miss Abernathy raised her hand. "These closures are by order of the mayor and at the suggestion of the United States Public Health Department. They will remain in ef-fect until the spread of the Spanish influenza is no longer a threat. Miss Elliot has announced our full compliance with this order. Therefore, the following rules apply to all students at St. Helen's

Hall: First, all day students and boarders with homes in the city or surrounding towns will be picked up immediately by authorized family members."

Grace reached across the narrow aisle and grabbed my hand. I thought she would squeeze the life out of it. I kept silent, holding on just as tight.

"Second, all boarders with homes outside Portland will remain on campus for the duration of the closure or until the arrival of an authorized family member. In this case, the student will meet her guardian by the main gates, as visitors will not be permitted on school grounds save approved deliverymen and medical personnel. If a student leaves the grounds without permission, she will not be allowed reentry under any circumstances." She paused, long enough to aim a pointed look toward the back of the class.

I snuck a glance over my shoulder at Margaret, who scowled at her textbook.

Miss Abernathy continued. "St. Helen's Hall will remain under—"

A violent sneeze erupted. Our heads swiveled. Louisa sat, frozen, before her hand flew up to cover a second sneeze. She produced a handkerchief and blew her nose.

"Off you go, Louisa," Miss Abernathy said quietly.

Louisa looked dismayed. "It was just the dust, Miss Abernathy. I—"

"I'm certain it was just the dust. But you are as aware of the rules as I am. Off you go."

I held my breath, filled with sympathy as Louisa clutched her book to her chest and marched toward the front of the room. Fanny held a handkerchief to her nose and leaned as far back as her chair would allow when Louisa passed. The door opened, then shut. My nose tickled and I dropped Grace's hand to rub it. I did not want to be the next person banished from the room.

Miss Abernathy turned back to the class, unsmiling. "As I was saying, St. Helen's will remain under quarantine until Miss Elliot and city officials deem it safe to reopen." She folded the paper in half, then in quarters. She touched the small cameo brooch pinned to her blouse. Every one of us raised our hands. Miss Abernathy focused on Grace.

"Miss Skinner."

"How long are the closures, Miss Abernathy?" Grace asked. "Days? Weeks? Surely there's an estimate."

"I'm sorry, Grace. It could be for just a few days. Or it could be weeks. At this time, we simply don't know."

Grace sat back, looking panicked.

Margaret raised her hand.

"Miss Kesey."

"My parents will be returning from Seattle soon, Miss Abernathy," Margaret said. "But our housekeeper is at home. And the rest of the staff. May I wait for them there?"

"You may not. It is absolutely out of the question. All students will be picked up by parents or guardians only. There will be no exceptions."

Margaret crossed her arms and glared at her desk.

I raised my hand.

"Miss Berry."

"Has something happened, Miss Abernathy?" I asked. "Since yesterday? Are things worse at Camp Lewis?"

"It *is* worse at the camp. But that isn't why schools are being closed." She hesitated; her gaze swept the room. "There are reports this morning of influenza here in the city."

Several desks away, Emmaline pressed a palm to her stomach and took deep breaths; inhaling through her nose, exhaling through her mouth, as though trying to inflate a paper sack. I could hear Miss Gillette in the next classroom, clapping her hands and demanding quiet.

"How many reports?" This time Margaret didn't bother to raise her hand.

Miss Abernathy had been a teacher at St. Helen's Hall for ten years. Not once in that entire time had she coddled her students. She didn't start now. She looked directly at Margaret.

"Two hundred," she said.

CHAPTER FIVE

Friday, October 11, 1918

A telegram for you, miss."

"Thank you, Mary."

The maid hurried down the hall. I shut the door. For once, I had the room entirely to myself. Hours had passed since Miss Elliot had dismissed us for who knows how long. Fanny's parents had already come to fetch her. The family was on its way back to Scappoose. Grace had gone downstairs to greet her father, who had just arrived from their home in Oswego. Margaret, like me, was trapped here until relatives arrived, but she'd said something about calling Harris and was nowhere in sight.

The Western Union telegram was printed on yellow paper. The address read: MISS CLEO BERRY, ST. HELEN'S HALL, PORT-LAND. The message was brief: AWARE OF CLOSURE. RETURNING EARLY. WILL SEND WORD ONCE ARRANGEMENTS ARE MADE. JACK.

I leaned against the door. Tears pricked my eyes. But for the first time since Miss Abernathy shared the horrible news, the tension in my shoulders eased. The trains must be safe if Jack and Lucy were coming back. I could not wait to see them. Their anniversary trip was ruined, and I was sorry for it. But I would breathe much, much easier once they were home.

An automobile horn blasted. I crossed the room and looked out the open window beside my bed. I was two floors up. Down below, on the wide expanse of lawn, chaos reigned. The rain had stopped, though the clouds remained dark and heavy. Fathers and drivers stumbled toward waiting automobiles, their arms laden with suitcases. Mothers collected their children, from the smallest students in the lower school to girls my own age. The scene reminded me of the final day of classes, right before summer vacation. Only it wasn't June, it was October. And not one person below was smiling.

Miss Elliot was easy to pick out of the crowd. She stood in the center of it all—white hair, black dress. Pressed against her side was Emily. And Greta, whose button eyes could be seen even from this distance. Directly below my window, six-year-old Anna Clarke struggled to free herself from her mother's iron grip.

"But I want to say goodbye to Emily, Mama!" Anna's cries carried up through my window. Her mother would not be swayed. When Anna continued to protest, Mrs. Clarke stopped, seized her daughter by the shoulders, and shook her. I could not hear what was said, but Anna finally followed with her head bowed low. Mrs. Clarke looked near tears.

I watched as the line of cars snaked around the circular driveway and through wrought-iron gates. My schoolmates departed, one by one. Whisked away to the safety and comfort of their homes.

Unlike me.

I threw the telegram onto my apple-green quilt and flopped beside it. As I did, a faint tinkling sounded. Puzzled, I looked around. My leather satchel hung from a post at the foot of the bed. There were only a few items in it, I remembered. Some money. My sketchbook. Pencils. A pack of Juicy Fruit.

A set of house keys.

I sat up. I lifted the satchel from the post, undid each clasp, and peered inside. There they were. On a small silver ring. Lying at the very bottom. Long seconds passed while I considered how much trouble I was about to get myself into.

I pulled the ring free and set the bag aside. There was one key for my front door, one for the back. One for the carriage house, which held two cars. One for Jack's office downtown. I swung the ring round and round on one finger, listening to the *jingle-jangle* of keys. Before I could change my mind, I dropped the ring back into the satchel and slung the strap over my head. I didn't bother with luggage. I was halfway across the room when the door opened.

It was Grace, still dressed in her school uniform but wearing a smart gray hat and gloves. "Cleo, I came to say good . . ." She trailed off, her eyes on my satchel. "Where are you going?"

I pulled her into the room before leaning out the door and peering down the hall. Deserted, thank goodness. I shut the door with a snap. So much for a quick escape.

"I'm going home."

The last thing I wanted to do was to stay here under quarantine. Barely a mile away, my house stood empty. Mrs. Foster was off visiting her son for another week or so. But Jack and Lucy were on their way. What was the harm in waiting for them there? I was eighteen, nearly, and I could manage on my own for two days. I *hated* living here.

Grace looked bewildered. "But there's no one at your home. Is there?"

"No." I held up both hands to stem her protest. "Jack and Lucy are on their way." I showed her the telegram. Grace snatched it from my fingers, her brows furrowing even further as she read Jack's message. "I'll wait for them at the house."

"Alone?"

"Shhh!" I glanced at the door. With any luck, I could lose myself in the crowd before anyone thought to wonder where I was. "Yes, alone. Please promise me you won't say anything."

"This is a terrible idea! You could be attacked by burglars. Or worse! You could die of the influenza and no one will know because you'll be all alone!"

"Grace . . ."

Grace shook her head. "No. You're coming with us. Father is waiting downstairs." She glanced about the room. "Where's your luggage?"

I wrapped my arms around her. "You know I can't go with you. Miss Elliot would never allow it. Besides, I can't leave the city." The Skinners were driving to their summer home in Florence. Grace's parents were convinced that the fresh sea air would stave off the worst of the epidemic. It was hours away by automobile. Jack would be angry enough when he discovered I wasn't at school. I didn't want to think about what he'd do if I left Portland.

Grace pulled away, unhappy. "You'll go straight home? You won't do anything foolish?"

"I won't," I said, exasperated. "What would I do?"

"What about provisions?" she pressed. "Do you have enough food? You'll have to arrange for milk delivery. And ice." Her frown deepened. "Your house is enormous, Cleo. I would be scared to death, staying there all by myself."

Grace was not helping.

"You make it sound like I'll be alone for a month!" I said. "The pantry is full, I'm sure, knowing Mrs. Foster. And I can always walk to the bakery and buy a sandwich if I need to. It will be like camping."

Grace looked unconvinced. "You've never camped a day in your life," she pointed out, before sighing. A great put-upon sigh. "You're sure?"

"I am." I tried to remember which dairy and ice service Mrs. Foster used. And what about firewood? Did we have enough? Who did I telephone for that? I could honestly say I'd never once given the purchase of firewood a thought.

Grace relented. "*Fine*. I'll keep your ridiculous secret. For now." A small stack of cream-colored note cards lay on her desk, beside a teacup filled with freshly sharpened pencils. Grace wrote on a card before handing it to me. "This is our address in Florence—"

I sighed. "I know your address, Grace."

Grace snatched my hand, set the card on my palm, and looked me straight in the eye. "Take it anyway," she ordered. "Will you promise to telephone if you change your mind? Or if you need help? Anything? I can take the Packard myself and be back here straightaway."

I folded the note in half and looked out the window. Grace's father stood by his car, frowning at a pocket watch. I thought of all that had happened today. I thought of Grace leaving. There was a lump in my throat the size of an apple.

"I promise," I said.

Grace sidled closer until our shoulders touched. "Miss El- liot is there," she said, pointing. "You see? With Emily and Miss Bishop." She looked at me, worry and indecision stamped on her face. "But I was just outside. No one is watching the back gates."

The gravel crunched beneath my feet as I made my way toward the south entrance. Grace was right — not a soul occupied the back lawn. I passed empty tennis courts and abandoned picnic tables and walked right through the gates. I'd just started to relax when I heard the rumble of an engine behind me. The sound grew louder and more ominous as it approached. I kept my gaze on my shoes and stifled a groan.

It had been too easy.

The car slowed beside me and stopped. The engine sputtered into silence. Left with no choice, I looked over my shoulder.

Margaret occupied the passenger seat of a shiny new roadster. She wore a moss-green coat and hat. She eyed my satchel, her expression disapproving. "Your brother is going to kill you, Cleo."

I glanced past her at the sandy-haired boy in the driver's seat. "You are hardly one to lecture," I said.

Harris leaned around Margaret with a sheepish grin. He had a wide, friendly face and ears that stood out even more after a recent haircut. "Afternoon, Cleo."

"Hello, Harris."

Margaret opened her door. "Come on." She scooted over to make room. "We'll take you home."

"No, it's fine. I feel like a walk."

Frowning, Margaret moved back across the seat. "Jack and Lucy are on their way home? You won't be alone for very long?"

"I won't." My own questions ran through my mind. *Where are you going? What will you do?* But I kept quiet, because I was hardly innocent. And because Harris would be heading off to Fort Stevens tomorrow.

Reaching into the car, I wrapped both arms around Margaret before giving her a kiss on the cheek. "You'll be careful?" I asked.

Margaret sniffled. "I will. You too, Cleo. Try not to do anything I wouldn't do."

I laughed. Stepping back, I looked at Harris, whom I had known since we were children. "Lucy and I will keep your mama company the next time we're in Salem, Harris. And I'm sure Jack will stop in on your father. Don't you worry about anything except coming home safe."

Harris's ears turned bright pink. "My parents will appreciate it. I'm obliged to you, Cleo." Margaret placed a hand on his arm.

I shut the door. As the car continued on its way, Margaret stuck her head out the window and waved. I waved back. Before they disappeared, I caught a final glimpse of green: green hat, green coat. And a rare wide smile. I dropped my hand and hurried down the path.

I never saw them again.

CHAPTER SIX

Friday, October 11, 1918

Oregonian! Get your paper here! 'Influenza Hits Portland! Mayor Shuts Down City!' Paper, paper! Paper, mister?"

I flipped a nickel toward the newsboy standing on the street corner. He was about ten, with a blue cap pulled over scruffy hair. The child caught the coin and thrust a newspaper my way, then pirouetted neatly and palmed a second nickel tossed from the opposite direction. With the paper tucked in my satchel, I made my way down Thirteenth Street.

Portland was a city of more than two hundred thousand residents, with a long, meandering river, the Willamette, bisecting it into east and west. St. Helen's Hall was located on the southwestern edge of the city; my house was north on King Street. I avoided a baby carriage. Dodged a delivery boy on a bicycle. And I felt as though I'd stepped into another world entirely.

It was the masks.

On the corner of Thirteenth and Jefferson, at the florist, Mr. Pressman held the door open for two elderly matrons. A red carnation was pinned to his lapel, as usual. But a white gauze mask covered his thin mustache and cheery smile. Startled, my gaze roamed over the crowd. I saw another one. And another. And there, the man with the cane. Another.

All around me, automobiles clamored for a share of the road alongside lumbering trucks, wooden carts, and the occasional horse-drawn buggy. A streetcar driver bore down upon unsuspecting pedestrians, oblivious to the indignant cries and raised fists left in his wake. I stared after the car, perplexed, until I realized it was a summer trolley put back into service. Unlike the cold-weather cars, summer trolleys had no doors, windows, aisles, or sides. Affixed to the rear of the streetcar was a sign that read, simply, SPIT SPREADS DEATH.

There was a new placard in the window of Hammond's Drug Store: SPANISH INFLUENZA REMEDIES. TRIED-AND-TRUE CURES, COMPLETELY EFFECTIVE. Directly below were displays of mustard tins, quinine jars, onion crates, and baskets filled with Vicks Vapo-Rub. Customers rushed in and out, and I could see Mr. and Mrs. Hammond through the window, frantically trying to fulfill orders. The druggist and his wife, too, were masked.

I passed a small stone church, chains wrapped around its front doors. By then panic had set in, hard and sharp.

I turned left, on Salmon Street, and quickly headed for home.

King Street was in a neighborhood set high in the west hills. Home to judges and lawyers, hoteliers and publishers, and one architect: Jack. My father had built our home, a mix of pale sandstone and English Tudor, when my brother was a baby. The house was big and rambling, with enough room for five children. I wondered sometimes if my parents had dreamed of a larger family.

I dashed up the front steps and let myself in. I dropped my satchel beside the umbrella stand and tugged my gloves free, setting them on the entryway table. The air smelled faintly of cigar smoke and furniture polish.

I looked about. To the right was the parlor with its grand piano and fireplace. To the left, a closed door led to Jack's study. Directly ahead, up a short flight of steps, was the formal dining room. Unlike the world outside, everything was in its place.

I stood in the center of the foyer, listening to a sound I'd been desperate to hear for weeks. Silence. Yet it did not thrill me the way I thought it would.

It was the sound of being completely and utterly alone.

That night a storm raged. The rain and wind rattled the windowpanes. The house creaked and moaned, like an old man rising from a chair. I lay in bed with the covers tight over my head. In total darkness, I regretted every Poe story ever read. Was sorry for every minute spent with Shelley's *Frankenstein*.

I pulled the covers down and sat up. Switching on the lamp, I checked to make sure Jack's old baseball bat still leaned against my night table within arm's reach. My bedroom was decorated in soft greens and yellows, with a small fireplace and a window seat piled high with pillows. I looked around to make sure nothing—or no one—lurked where they shouldn't.

My satchel sat by the door. After climbing out of bed, I padded barefoot across the wooden floor and fished the newspaper I had yet to read from the bag. The room was chilly, my fire having died out hours ago. I rushed back across the room and flung myself beneath the covers.

A package of shortbread cookies lay open on the night table, and I helped myself to one. I'd found Mrs. Foster's list of grocers in a kitchen drawer by the telephone. But the provisions I'd ordered, including ice for the icebox, would not be delivered until morning. There were plenty of packaged foods and canned goods in the pantry, though. My dinner had consisted of shortbread cookies, canned peaches, and a glass of water. Grace was right. This was as close to camping as I was likely to get.

I unfolded the *Oregonian,* smoothing it onto my yellow quilt. Influenza and war dominated the front page. MAYOR ORDERED TO CLOSE UP CITY. TICONDEROGA SUNK, SCORES KILLED. WOUNDED

MARINE ROBBED. I read one unsettling story after another before a tiny article near the bottom captured my attention.

The American Red Cross has issued an urgent plea that all graduate nurses, practical nurses, women with nursing experience, and Red Cross nurses' aides enroll for immediate service in combating the Spanish influenza. Also needed are members of the community willing to canvass neighborhoods, distributing prevention literature and helping to locate and transport unattended cases to area hospitals. Those with automobiles are particularly encouraged to make themselves known. The Red Cross is mobilizing every possible resource from the Atlantic to the Pacific. To this end, it asks that all available nursing material in and around Portland enroll at the Public Auditorium.

Unattended cases.

I stared at the words until they started to blur. What did they mean? Were people lying in their homes with no one to care for them? Too ill to telephone for help? Children too?

I leaned against my headboard, watching as lightning flashed across the sky, listening to the deep roll of thunder. Common sense told me not to even consider it. I was in enough trouble as it was. Others would help, surely. Wouldn't they?

I read the article a second time, feeling as if it had been written for my eyes only. I didn't have any nursing experience. Absolutely none. But I had two automobiles. Jack's Packard was parked in our old carriage house, alongside the Ford that Mrs. Foster used for the market and other errands. Last summer Jack had taught me how to master the Ford's testy hand crank and how to keep from rolling backwards down Marquam Hill. It had taken some doing, and it was the only time I'd ever heard my brother scream, but I could drive either car now, easily.

I shoved the newspaper beneath my bed, then turned off the lamp and pulled the covers to my chin. I stayed awake for hours. In the darkness, I no longer thought of Dr. Frankenstein's monster or of burglars creeping up the stairs.

I thought of my parents.

Of my mother and father, and that last terrifying night in the carriage. Twelve years had passed, but I still knew exactly what it was to be an unattended case.

CHAPTER SEVEN

Saturday, October 12, 1918

First name?"

"Cleo. C-L-E-O."

"Last?"

"Berry."

"Age?"

"Seventeen."

The nurse paused. "Seventeen?" she asked.

"Yes."

"Hmm." She tapped her pencil against the tabletop.

I forced myself not to fidget. It was midmorning. The rain had finally stopped, though the clouds overhead were dark and gloomy.

I stood just outside the Public Auditorium on Third Street.

Only a year old, it was the most important art venue in the city, used for operas and ballets, symphonies and musicals, comedy acts, exhibitions, and lectures. The building was constructed of pale concrete, with eleven marble terraces carved into the main façade. Shallow granite steps ran its length. It was here, at the foot of the stairs, that the nurse sat behind a skirted table. She was Lucy's age, in her early thirties, with auburn hair, blue eyes, and a brisk, no-nonsense demeanor. Beside her was another nurse, at least twenty years older and stout. Both women were dressed in white, with red crosses stitched onto their sleeves and hats. Gauze face masks, also a pristine white, dangled from their necks.

The second nurse frowned. "She's very young, Hannah."

"Kate is seventeen," Hannah answered, the faintest Irish lilt to her voice.

The second nurse *tsk*ed. "Katherine's been helping her mother for years. She knows her way around the wards. This child . . ."

They spoke as if I were invisible, and I felt my good intentions seep out of my pores onto the sidewalk. I was dressed in a long navy skirt and matching coat with a round collar and slightly flared hem. I knew I looked to be exactly what I was. A foolish schoolgirl, out where she shouldn't be.

The ladies standing in line behind me surely heard every word. My cheeks burned. I glanced back. There were eight of them. Eight. Was that all? They were dressed for the morning chill and were much older than I. Their expressions ranged from curious to disapproving. I turned around, listening to the nurses debate whether to keep me or send me packing.

My embarrassment faded, replaced by annoyance. I'd rushed down here as soon as the deliverymen had left the house. The iceman had arrived a full hour late, and I'd spent the entire time worrying that Miss Elliot would arrive on my doorstep breathing fire and waving expulsion papers. Reaching into my coat pocket, I felt the article I'd clipped rustle beneath my fingertips. The Red Cross had asked for drivers. They had sounded desperate. If there was an age requirement, they should have been more specific.

I lifted my chin. "The newspaper said you needed volunteers with automobiles," I said. "To canvass the neighborhoods."

Hannah straightened. "You have an automobile?"

"Yes." I gestured toward the row of identical black cars parked across the street.

The plump nurse frowned even more. "But—"

Hannah interrupted. "I understand, Mrs. Howard. I do. But as you can see . . ." She tipped her head at the queue behind me, giving me a faintly apologetic look. "We do not have the luxury of turning down help when it's offered."

Mrs. Howard shook her head and turned away, beckoning the next person in line.

Hannah reached beneath the table and handed me a white

cloth bag. I peeked in. It was filled to the brim with neatly bound pamphlets and masks.

"Some patients are ill for several days before being found in their homes," she explained as I glanced at the pamphlet. Its cover read INFLUENZA: HOW TO AVOID IT—HOW TO CARE FOR THOSE WHO HAVE IT. "We need volunteers who will walk the neighborhoods. Knock on doors, find those who are sick, and call for help."

I nodded. It sounded simple enough.

Hannah pointed at the bag. "Every person should receive a mask, and each household should get a copy of our influenza care guide. It's not necessary for you to wear your own mask outdoors. Fresh air is best. But we ask that you please wear one when you enter a home. And always when you're in the hospital wards."

I tied the white fabric around my neck. "Where should I start?" I asked.

"There've been several reports of flu on Caruthers Street," she said. "Just south of here. I'll have you start there. The addresses are in your bag. You can just cross them off as you go and bring the list to me before you head home for the day. And remember, if there is family at home who can care for the ill, then by all means leave them to it." She glanced over her shoulder at the Auditorium. "This hospital is mainly for those who have nowhere else to go. Otherwise, we'd be overrun. We might be overrun as it is.

"We don't have extra uniforms, unfortunately. But, here, hold out your arm." She stood and wrapped a white armband around my right coat sleeve. The brassard was about four inches wide, with a red cross emblazoned in the center. After a few adjustments, she secured the armband with two pins. "So people will know why you're looking in their windows," she explained. "It wouldn't do to have you shot."

I blinked, waiting for her to laugh at her joke. When she did not, I responded with a cautious, "Oh."

Hannah sat. "I have to warn you, telephone service is becoming more and more unreliable. And many families don't even own a telephone. *And* there's only one ambulance service in town. Sometimes they don't show up right away."

I stared at her. "Then . . . what would you have me do?"

"Do what we all do in times like these," she said. "Hazard a guess. I'm Hannah Flynn. Good luck to you, Cleo Berry." Leaning slightly to one side, she looked around me.

"Next, please."

I stopped the car, waiting as the elderly man shuffled across the street. He was dressed in a black suit and hat, and had a wiry beard that tumbled to his chest. On the sidewalk, a group of similarly attired gentlemen gathered outside a synagogue. The old man raised one papery hand in greeting as he headed in their direction.

South Portland was home to thousands of Jewish and Italian families. Around me, family-run businesses lined both sides of Second Street. Merchants had flung open their doors, hoping to entice customers with corned beef and pastrami, bagels and challah, cheeses and salami and green olives soaked in brine. A small tailoring shop stood dark and shuttered, but beside it a kosher butcher did a brisk business. Men and women went about their day. It would have looked like a normal morning, had it not been for the masks.

An impatient horn blasted, startling me, and I saw that the old man had made it safely across. I was blocking the street. Chagrined, I stepped on the gasoline pedal. The car lurched forward.

Several blocks later, I turned onto Caruthers Street. Old homes and modest apartment buildings came into view. Squinting up at the addresses, I stopped at the end of the street. Then I reached for my bag, jumped out, and hoped for the best.

The house was several stories high — narrow, with a weed-filled yard and sagging porch. Brown paint had flecked off the sides in such quantities that the house had taken on the appearance of a speckled egg. I climbed the steps and knocked on the door. A child's squeal rang out, followed by shushing noises. The door opened a sliver, just enough for me to glimpse a woman with a thin, suspicious face. I smiled.

"Yes?"

"Good morning." I held up a pamphlet. "I'm with the Red Cross. My name is Cleo Berry. We're in your neighborhood today distributing information on the Spanish influenza and handing out face masks for your household."

"How much does it cost?" the woman asked, still frowning.

"Why, nothing. It's free."

"Oh." The door opened further. The woman wore a threadbare yellow housedress, printed with tiny red flowers. A toddler, dressed only in a diaper, clutched the woman's dress in two little fists. I could not tell if the child was a boy or a girl.

"Hello," I said to the baby, who ducked shyly between dress folds. I looked back at the woman. "How many masks would you like?" I asked.

"Well, there's just my husband and me. And Bertie here." She gave the child a doubtful look. "We don't need one for him, I guess. He'd never keep it on. So two."

I handed the woman two masks and a pamphlet. "This will tell you how to care for your family if they get sick. And where to find help if you need it."

The woman flipped through the brochure. A mottled flush crept up her neck. "Can you tell me what it says?" she asked, then hastily added, "Just the important bits, is all. I . . . I'm not too good at reading."

I hoped my surprise didn't show. The woman looked embarrassed enough. "I can, certainly. Here." I reached for the pamphlet and read:

INFLUENZA: HOW TO AVOID IT — HOW TO CARE FOR THOSE WHO HAVE IT. THE USUAL SYMPTOMS ARE INFLAMED AND WATERY EYES, BACKACHE, HEADACHE, MUSCULAR PAIN, NOSEBLEEDS, AND FEVER. PROTECT OTHERS BY SNEEZING OR COUGHING INTO HANDKERCHIEFS OR CLOTHS, WHICH SHOULD BE BOILED OR BURNED. KEEP AWAY FROM CROWDED PLACES. INSIST THAT WHOEVER GIVES YOU FOOD OR WATER OR ENTERS THE SICKROOM FOR ANY OTHER PURPOSE SHALL WEAR A GAUZE MASK. MAKE FULL USE OF ALL AVAILABLE SUNSHINE; WALK IN THE FRESH AIR DAILY. ISOLATE YOUR PATIENTS. SLEEP WITH YOUR WINDOWS OPEN. OBTAIN AT LEAST SEVEN HOURS OF SLEEP EVERY TWENTY-FOUR HOURS. EAT PLENTY OF GOOD, CLEAN FOOD. SMALL CHILDREN ARE PARTICULARLY VULNERABLE. SEE TO IT THAT YOUR CHILDREN ARE KEPT WARM AND DRY, BOTH NIGHT AND DAY.

I read the pamphlet front to back. When I looked up, the woman had paled. She stared down at her child in his diaper, and at the goose bumps pimpling his skin. She grabbed him up in her arms before snatching the pamphlet from my hand.

"Thank you," she said, and closed the door in my face.

✦ ✦ ✦

I trudged up the pathway toward the next house. Unlike most of the homes on the street, someone had taken good care of the simple one-story clapboard. Fresh white paint brightened the exterior, and, beneath my feet, the porch gleamed glossy and black. I knocked, then took a step back and waited. There was no answer. I knocked again, harder this time. Still no answer. Feeling self-conscious, I peered through the only available window, set to the right of the door.

A flowered settee stood against the opposite wall, a white crocheted throw spread over one arm. Two chairs, heavy and dark, crowded around an ancient piano, its top littered with framed photographs and tiny animal figurines. An unlit fireplace stood in the corner. The parlor looked charming and cozy and cluttered, but there was no sign anyone was home.

I stood there dithering and wondered what to do next. Hannah's advice to *hazard a guess* was not the least bit helpful. The family could be at work, or at the grocer's, or out of town for all I knew. Or they could be lying just out of sight, unable to summon help. Apprehensive, I thought of the gun Jack kept in his study. A gun he wouldn't think twice about firing should a stranger stroll, uninvited, into his home. But I knew I wouldn't rest easy until I had assured myself that the house was empty.

I gave the door one last rap, calling, "Hello? Is anyone home?" When my third attempt was met with silence, I threw a furtive look over my shoulder. The street was quiet. Not a single automobile or truck occupied the road. I reached down and tried the doorknob. Locked.

I retraced my steps and skirted the house. Other than a rag rug hanging from a clothesline, the small enclosed yard was empty. I dropped my bag beside an old rocking chair on the back porch. Cupping my hands to each side of my face, I peered through a window.

My eyes adjusted to the dim interior. It was a kitchen. In the center of the room stood a breakfast table and three chairs. A fourth chair was pushed up against the countertop. White cupboards hung open, exposing the pantry's assortment of plates, saucers, and bowls. A cereal box lay on its side on the countertop, toasted oats spilled all over the linoleum floor.

I looked at the chair, at the cereal, and felt the rapid beating of my heart. Only a child would use a chair to reach the cupboards. Why would he need to? Where were his parents? For that matter, where was the child?

I pounded on the back door with my fist. I rattled the knob. To my astonishment, it turned in my hand. I pushed the door open and raced down a short hall. There were two rooms, both with doors firmly shut. I stopped in front of the first one. Lifted my hand. Dropped it. The temptation to run away was fierce. An odor, faint but ominous, enveloped me, causing the skin on my face to tighten. The only sound came from my own shallow breathing. Taking a deep breath, I opened the door and stepped inside.

The smell of vomit and dirty diapers filled the air. My hand flew to my mouth.

It was a bedroom, dim and silent. Two bodies lay on the bed. A woman in a white nightgown was twisted in the sheets, her long dark hair matted with sweat. Dried blood crusted her nose and lips. Her face was the color of chalk. A little boy, no more than three, curled into her side. He had thrown up all over his blue pajamas.

A whimper emerged from my throat. Trying not to panic, I approached the bed. I felt the woman's cheek with the back of my hand. She was on fire, her breath so shallow I had to concentrate just to see the rise and fall of her chest. The child didn't feel nearly as hot, and he breathed easier than his mother. I sent up a tiny prayer of thanks. They needed help, and quickly, but for now at least they were alive.

I ran to the kitchen. A telephone sat on a small table near the door. I snatched up the receiver and waited, only to be met with silence.

"Damn, damn, damn!" Dropping the phone, I raced back into the bedroom, stopping dead in my tracks when I realized there was a third person in the room. How could I have failed to see?

A wooden cradle lay on the floor, on the far side of the bed. Kneeling, I placed my hand against the infant's splotchy cheek. Alive. I started to pick the baby up. As I did, a soiled diaper slid down dimpled legs and dropped into the cradle with a resounding *plop*.

Frantic, I glanced into the hall, willing someone to appear and take charge. A police officer, a neighbor, my brother. Anyone. I wanted nothing more than to crouch in a corner and wail. But no one was coming. I was entirely on my own. Me, and three unattended cases.

I gathered the infant, whom I discovered to be a girl, close in one arm. I scooped up the boy with the other. Then I spared one last look for their unconscious mother.

"I'm sorry. I will send help. I promise," I whispered.

I stumbled to the front of the house, nearly dropping the baby as I fumbled with the doorknob. I half ran, half staggered down the path toward the car parked across the street. The roads were still empty. I looked toward the first house I'd visited. The woman with the yellow housedress watched me from a window. Our eyes met through the glass. She yanked the curtains closed, leaving me dumbfounded. I settled the children as carefully as I could onto the rear seat. I turned the crank at the front of the car, jumped into the driver's seat, and started the engine.

We were off.

It was only then that I realized how badly my hands were shaking.

CHAPTER EIGHT

Saturday, October 12, 1918

The car came to an abrupt stop outside the Auditorium, sending a tall, dark-haired young man leaping out of the way onto the sidewalk. Brown liquid flew from the paper cup in his hands, soaking the front of a white lab coat. He looked down at the dripping stains, then turned to glare at me through the windshield.

"Hey—!"

Ignoring him, I jumped out and reached for the baby. She felt as if she were being cooked from the inside out. With her head cupped in my palm, I whirled to face the stranger. He marched my way with a scowl on his face but stopped in his tracks when he saw what I held, indignation dissolving into astonishment.

"Please help!" I stumbled over a sobbing breath. "There are two of them!"

The stranger tossed his cup. I moved aside so he could lean into the rear seat, where the boy lay sprawled and feverish. He checked the child's pulse and muttered something under his breath.

I hovered, craning my neck to see around him. "Will he be all right?"

"I don't know." Lifting the boy in his arms, he backed out, then reached over and placed two fingers on the baby's neck. I inhaled sharply. Ugly, puckered flesh marred the skin of the young man's right hand, above the knuckles. Was it a bullet wound? Had he been shot? He caught me staring—his eyes were the clear, crystal green of sea glass. I didn't even have time to be embarrassed. Sparing me one quick, unsmiling look, he said, "Let's go!" before racing up the steps toward the main doors.

I ran after him, the baby clutched tight. There were people coming and going. Heads swiveled before we burst through the metal doors into the ticket lobby. Two white-clad nurses, masked, surrounded us in an instant. One rushed after the stranger, who had gone through the interior doors. The other I recognized as the older nurse from the volunteer table—the one who had thought I was far too young to be here. How I wished that Hannah had listened to her.

"Let me have her," she ordered. I gave up my hold on the baby. And watched as they too disappeared through the glass doors.

Dazed, I sagged against a wall. The lobby was long and narrow, with black-and-white squares tiling the floor like a chessboard. Two ticket windows were positioned at opposite ends of the room. Chairs had been brought in, pushed against walls, every one of them occupied. A woman with a sleeping baby in her arms. Two men in sailor uniforms. There was a priest, a police officer, an old woman with a lap full of knitting. The ticket lobby had become a waiting room.

A cup of water appeared before me.

It was Hannah Flynn, her brows knit in concern. "Cleo, was it?" she asked. When I nodded, she said, "Here, drink this. You look like you've had quite the day so far."

I snatched the cup and gulped down the entire contents before coming up for air. An ambulance siren wailed in the distance. "Thank you," I said after I'd regained my breath. "The children. They'll be fine, won't they?"

Hannah glanced toward the glass doors. "I couldn't say just yet. Why don't we give Lieutenant Parrish some time with them, and then I'll see how they are."

I stared at her. "Lieutenant? You mean . . . he's not a real doctor?"

Hannah shook her head. "Edmund is a medical student."

I'd just handed those children off to a *student*. Someone barely older than I was. "I don't understand," I said. "Where are the doctors?"

"There are a few here," Hannah said. "But many have been

sent to the military infirmaries. Even more are abroad." My feelings must have been written plainly on my face, because she added, "I know. But this flu is new to all of us, which means Edmund knows as much as I do. As much as any of the doctors. We're all students here. Every last one of us."

Her words were the opposite of comforting. I hoped she kept those thoughts away from her patients. I tossed the cup into a bin. Above it was a handwritten notice that read: *Visitors allowed in the wards only under extreme circumstances.*

Lieutenant Edmund Parrish. Whoever he was, I hoped he knew what he was doing. Those poor children and their mother . . . I gasped. *Their mother!*

"We have to go back!" I said, horrified at myself for forgetting. "I couldn't carry their mother. I need—"

"Come with me." Hannah strode toward the entrance doors. I hurried after her. We clattered down the steps toward an ambulance parked directly behind my car, the engine still running. Two uniformed men sprinted by in the opposite direction. Balanced between them was a teenage boy on a stretcher. I glimpsed a wan face and dull, listless eyes and had to force myself not to stare.

Hannah circled the truck until she stood in front of the driver's open door. The man at the wheel had brown hair threaded with gray and skin that sagged like an old bloodhound's. A pencil was lodged above one ear. He used a second pencil to scribble on a notepad.

He looked up at our approach and scratched his beard. "I've seen that look before, Hannah. I can guess what you're after."

Hannah smiled. "And you would be correct, Mr. Briggs. You won't mind moving this one to the top of your list? It's an emergency."

Mr. Briggs looked exasperated. "They're all emergencies," he said, but relented. "Whattya got?"

"A woman at . . ." Hannah turned toward me, eyebrows raised. I gave them the address. Mr. Briggs wrote it down.

"Got it." He tucked the small notebook in his shirt pocket.

I stepped forward. "Mr. Briggs, she wasn't awake when I left, but the front door should be unlocked. The back door, too." I had also forgotten my new bag, filled with pamphlets and masks, on the back porch. *And* I had neglected to pull up my own mask before I charged into the house. I hoped I didn't look as incompetent as I felt.

There was a sympathetic gleam in Mr. Briggs's eyes. I had a feeling he knew exactly what I was thinking. "Both doors open," he said. "Good. Saves us the trouble of breaking them down ourselves."

I heard a loud thump. The men had jumped into the back with the empty stretcher. Hannah and I stepped away as Mr. Briggs swung his door shut. A siren pierced the air, and before I knew it, the ambulance sped down the street and careened around a corner.

I turned to Hannah. "Thank you," I said.

She placed her hands on her hips and studied me. "Hmm."

I looked down and grimaced. My navy coat hung open, revealing a white shirtwaist smeared with stains I had no wish to identify. I lifted the sleeve and sniffed, remembering too late the baby's bare bottom. My eyes watered. Hannah's lips curved. Behind us, a door slammed against the concrete wall. Startled, we looked toward the top of the staircase.

"No! I'm leaving. Don't you try to stop me, Kate!" A young woman bolted down the steps, dressed in a serviceable brown coat and hat. Close on her heels was a girl, about my age, dressed in a yellow shirtwaist and slim brown skirt. She wore no coat. They were obviously related, both of them pretty and slender, with brown hair and rosy cheeks.

The second girl, Kate, looked infuriated. "Oh, for heaven's sakes, Ruby! It will get better. You wanted to help."

Ruby's voice was shrill. "They're beyond help! I'm not about to die for a stranger. And you shouldn't either!" She brushed past us, jostling Hannah, but did not stop.

Kate stopped beside us and threw up her hands. "How am I supposed to get home?" she hollered at the departing figure. Ruby ignored her. We watched her wrench open the door of a battered old truck and drive away.

"Well, she lasted a full hour at least," Hannah said, resigned.

Kate looked embarrassed. "I don't know why she wanted to come in the first place. My sister's never been very good around blood. I'm sorry, Hannah."

Hannah rubbed the back of her neck with one hand, and for the first time I noticed the shadows under her blue eyes. "More will come, and stay. Kate, did you bring a change of clothing with you?"

"Yes. Why?"

"Could you spare a blouse for Cleo? She's had her own interesting time of it."

Skeptical, my gaze dropped to Kate's bosom, far more generous than mine. I would feel swallowed up in anything she owned. From the look on her face, I knew she agreed.

"I'll find something," Kate said, extending her hand. "I'm Katherine Bennett. Kate."

I took it, noticing for the first time that I was missing my right glove. When had that happened?

"Cleo Berry," I said. "I would be grateful."

I saw the instant the stench reached her. Kate opened her mouth to say something and then snapped it shut. She dropped my hand and stepped back.

"Whew!" she said.

"I'm sorry." Unable to bear it, I peeled off my remaining glove and shoved it in a skirt pocket, then shrugged out of my coat. It made no difference. I would need a new shirtwaist, a new coat, and a bar of strong-smelling soap.

"Well, enough with the pleasantries," Hannah said. She turned and started up the stairs. "Let's get you freshened up and back to work, shall we?"

I was no stranger to the Public Auditorium. Jack, Lucy, and I had attended a performance of Verdi's *Rigoletto* just last month. Walking onto the main floor, I saw that the first- and second-tier balconies remained unchanged. The red velvet stage curtain was drawn. And high above our heads, the same five crystal chandeliers lit the room.

But nothing else was as I remembered.

Gone was the Auditorium's rich, patterned carpeting, now covered over with wooden floorboards. The red chairs were also missing, replaced by metal cots arranged in ten rows. I counted ten beds per row. Add to that the cots crowded into the orchestra pit—one hundred and twenty beds, approximately. The pipe organ, usually housed in the pit, was nowhere to be seen.

Gone too were the elegant men and women out for an evening's entertainment, dressed in fine silks and jewels. Instead, doctors, nurses, and volunteers, all masked, circled the infirmary, monitoring the sick with brisk efficiency.

Hannah, Kate, and I walked down an aisle, my filthy coat

clutched in one hand. I could not help it. I gawked, mesmerized by the men, women, and children lying hollow-eyed and feeble beneath white sheeting. The sound of misery suffocated me, an unsettling symphony of rattling coughs and unchecked moaning.

I scanned the room, but there was no sign of the lieutenant or the two children. We passed a soldier, still in his uniform, who hacked up blood onto a towel while a nurse gripped his shoulders. Others lay unmoving on their beds. They had a peculiar bluish cast to their skin. For some, the faintest stroke of color slashed across the cheekbones. But others were so dark they appeared almost black. What was causing it? Bruising? Had they fallen?

"There are so many," I said through my mask.

Hannah looked somber. "There are more at St. Vincent's," she said. "And they're setting up tents outside County Hospital and Good Samaritan. They're already running out of room." She stopped beside one bed, examining a blond girl who looked to be about ten.

I turned to Kate as we waited in the aisle. "Have you been here all morning?" I asked.

Kate shook her head. "Since last night," she answered. "My sister Waverley is a nurse at St. Vincent's. She came by the house, saying the Red Cross needed help and lots of it. My sister Etta is volunteering at County. Ruby, as you know, is useless. And my younger brothers and sisters are at home with my mother, helping with the pneumonia jackets and bandages."

Briefly, I wondered how many siblings Kate had before my thoughts returned to the patients. "Are those bruises?" I whispered, gesturing discreetly across the way toward a young man.

Kate followed my gaze. "He has cyanosis," she whispered back. At my blank look, she added, "It means his lungs are failing, and he doesn't have enough oxygen in his blood. It can turn a person's skin blue or purple. Sometimes even black. At least that's what Hannah says."

It sounded terrifying. "Will it go away? Once they get better?"

Kate glanced sideways at Hannah, who leaned over the child with a stethoscope. She kept her voice low. "Dr. McAbee has never seen anyone with cyanosis recover. And he's been a physician for forty years."

I turned to look at the man again, certain I'd misheard. "But . . . there are at least a dozen people here who look like that," I said.

"There are thirty-one," Kate said.

I didn't have a chance to respond. Hannah tucked the girl's blanket around her and straightened. Kate and I exchanged a look. The three of us continued down the aisle. This time I tried harder not to look at the patients.

Something else was bothering me. Most of the cots here were

occupied. And extra room was being prepared at St. Vincent's, Multnomah County, and Good Samaritan. I did a quick mental count. "We were told there were two hundred sick in the whole city," I said. How many patients were they expecting?

"There *were* two hundred," Hannah replied. "But that was yesterday. There are at least twice that now. And those are just the ones that have been reported."

I stopped in the center of the aisle. Two hundred yesterday, at least four hundred today. What did that mean for tomorrow? Or next week? And what about me? How long would it be before I ended up on one of those cots?

Surrounded by the smell of antiseptic and a coppery sweet scent I recognized as blood, I realized I could not do this. I did not want to be a patient here. I did not want to die. I should have remained at school, where it was safe and isolated. I should have listened to my brother.

Hannah and Kate were three cots down the aisle before they realized I had not followed.

Hannah turned. "What . . . ?" She took one look at my face and fell silent.

"I'm sorry." I backed away, slowly, toward the main doors. Mortification welled up inside me. "I'm very sorry. I can't stay here."

Sympathy flickered in Kate's eyes, but Hannah's expression gave away nothing.

"I understand," Hannah said. "Thank you for your help today. It was good to meet you, Cleo Berry." She turned on her heel and walked off. Kate followed.

I watched them go, wondering if some people were simply born brave and others not, and that was that. Or maybe Hannah Flynn and Kate Bennett were just crazy. Knowing the risks, one had to be crazy to remain here.

"Aren't you frightened?" I asked, my voice small, barely audible.

They heard me anyway and turned. A nurse and a doctor hustled by, each in the opposite direction. It was Hannah who answered.

"Of course I'm frightened," she said quietly. "And so is Kate. And everyone else here. But these people need help. If not me, then who?"

I thought about the baby I'd carried into the Auditorium only a little while ago. On a nearby cot, a woman struggled onto her elbows. The noise she made was terrible. Wild and rough at the same time, like a cat grappling with a massive hairball. An empty bucket lay on the floor. I dived for it, thrusting it forward just as she leaned over the side and retched. Revulsion filled me. But so did pity. Eventually, the woman fell back against the pillow, her breathing labored. Hannah leaned over her, clucking and soothing. I moved away to give her room.

Kate stood at the foot of the bed, holding the coat I'd dropped. She eyed my shirtwaist. Additional chunks of vomit covered the fabric, reminding me, disgustingly, of Margaret's nectarine pits.

I looked at Kate, at Hannah, at the bucket filled with vomit, at the endless rows of patients. I took a deep breath. Gathering up the tattered remnants of my courage, I asked, "May I still borrow that blouse?"

CHAPTER NINE

Saturday, October 12, 1918

The smell of frying cabbage and sausages could not mask the odor wafting through the hall. Someone had used the stairwell as a toilet. I wrinkled my nose and knocked on a door with peeling green paint.

I was back on Caruthers Street in an old, dilapidated apartment building. I had no idea what tomorrow would bring. Likely, I would be sitting in Jack's study with my head hanging low. Listening as my brother yelled and Lucy stood by looking thoroughly disappointed.

Today, however, I would finish what I'd started.

Kate had led me to a bathroom and produced a fresh blue shirtwaist that fit surprisingly well. It belonged to her sister Ruby, and I was welcome to keep it, she had said. There was still no sign of Lieutenant Parrish or the children. But before I left the

Auditorium, two familiar stretcher-bearers had swept onto the main floor. They carried the children's mother, still unconscious, her long dark hair trailing off the sides. I watched as they disappeared through a door leading to an adjacent assembly room and wondered if that was where they treated the critical cases. But looking around, how could it get any worse than this?

I'd stopped by the house to retrieve my bag from the back porch. Also, to make sure the house was locked up tight. Then I'd continued knocking on doors. I found a woman, mildly ill with the flu, but her husband and mother were both home to care for her. I left them to it. Several knocks went unanswered, though neighbors confirmed the occupants were seen leaving for work earlier in the day. I distributed most of the masks and brochures. Overall, the last few hours had been duller than dull, and I was grateful for it.

This building was the last one on the street. With only a few apartments left, I glanced at my bracelet watch. It was nearly three o'clock. I was starving, though after all that I'd seen and smelled today, I was surprised I still had an appetite. I would finish here and find some lunch. And then I would head back to the Auditorium and learn, finally, what had become of that poor family.

It took a moment before I realized no one had answered my knock. I tried again. A heavy object thumped against the thin wood, sending me hopping back with a yelp. From the other side of the door came a voice, deep and irate. "Go on! Get lost! What do I have to do to get some sleep around here?" There was another thud. Then silence.

I pressed my hand against my chest and waited for my heartbeat to settle. I walked to the last door and knocked. To my surprise, it swung open fast and wide.

"Well, hello." I smiled behind my mask, which I hated already. It itched. I suspected my face would develop a rash before too long.

The little girl before me was about eight, with messy brown braids and a blue dress. A small cloth bag hung from a string around her neck. The contents of the pouch were easy to identify. The smell of camphor balls permeated the air, so potent my eyes stung.

The child stared up at me with interest. Or, rather, she stared at the white and red armband I'd removed from my coat and pinned to the sleeve of my shirtwaist. "Are you a nurse, miss?"

The smile slid right off my face. "I'm not," I said. My eyes darted over her head. The apartment was small; it looked like the space was used as a combined parlor, kitchen, and dining room. A single grimy window remained shut. I didn't see a telephone, and there was no one else about. I looked down at the child. "Why do you ask? Do you need a nurse?"

"I think so." She looked over her shoulder to where a door stood open at the opposite end of the room. "Mateo's been in his room all day. I shake him, but he won't get up."

"Show me." I dropped my bag just inside the door and followed her, then stopped in the bedroom doorway, heartsick but unsurprised.

Sitting on the floor with his back resting against the foot of a bed was a boy of about ten. He was dressed in blue knickerbockers. Thin arms dangled on bent knees. The pouch hanging from his neck, identical to the girl's, had not fulfilled its promise. He looked up at our entrance, his heavily lashed brown eyes bright with fever.

The girl rushed to sit beside him. Tucking her arm into his, she looked up at me, fearful. "He's very hot."

I knelt beside them. Mateo mumbled something incomprehensible as I rested a hand against his cheek. I felt the familiar panic rising and tamped it down. I needed to be calm. Or at least pretend. I was the oldest person in the room. The adult.

"What is your name?" I asked the girl.

"Francesca Bassi."

"Will your parents be home soon, Francesca?"

She shook her head. "There's just Papa and Mateo and me. Papa's at the shipyard."

I sat back on my heels, thinking. Mateo had to go to a hospital. It would be easier to take him myself rather than search the building for a telephone. But I didn't want to take the little girl with me. To expose her any more than necessary. I couldn't leave her here alone. What should I do? "Listen to me, Francesca—"

"Buongiorno?" A woman's voice drifted in from the other room.

"Elena!" Francesca leaped to her feet, dislodging her brother's head so it flopped back against the bed. The girl ran from the room. Mateo began a slow lean to one side, and I grasped his shoulders with both hands, holding him upright. Fire seeped through his jacket, frightening me.

"Dio mio! Mateo!" A woman in a green dress stood in the doorway, staring at us in horror. She had curly black hair and wore a green dress. Francesca clung to her skirts.

Relief surged through me. "Are you a neighbor?" I asked. "A friend?"

"Sì, sì," the woman stammered, wide-eyed. "I am Elena Tolemei. I am a friend to Signor Bassi."

It was good enough. "I need to take Mateo to the hospital. Will you stay with Francesca until her father comes home?"

"Yes. Of course." Elena did not move from the doorway but instead wrapped both arms around Francesca. Her gaze was riveted on Mateo. "It is the influenza?"

"I think so." I gave Mateo a small shake. He jerked upright, for an instant, before slumping.

I leaned closer. "Mateo. I can't carry you. Can you try and walk for me?"

Elena came over and crouched on Mateo's other side. She smoothed his untidy black hair with her fingers. The boy stirred, opening his eyes. He mumbled something.

"Mateo?" I prodded.

"*Sí*, I can walk." He slurred his words. "*Certamente!* For I am Tarzan, king of the beasts!" His eyes closed.

Elena and I looked at each other, dismayed. The stories from the East Coast came rushing back to me. Patient after patient. Delirium.

"Please, help me pull him up," I said.

We managed to half coax, half drag Mateo to his feet. I snatched my bag off the floor before we left the apartment. We led him down three floors of dim, rank stairwell and into the gray daylight. Francesca trailed behind us.

With Mateo stowed in the rear seat, I turned the hand crank before climbing into the car. I started the engine, then looked at Elena through the open window.

"I'm going to take him to County," I said, raising my voice to be heard over the engine. Multnomah County, just a few blocks south on Hooker Street, was closer than the Auditorium. I had completely forgotten that fact during my earlier panic with the two children. "And I'll try to find his father. Do you know the name of the shipyard?"

Elena clutched Francesca's hand and nodded. "It is the Columbia River shipyard." She pointed east. "It is just there, near the bridge."

"And his name?"

"Nicolo Bassi. He is an assemblyman," Elena said. "*Scusa, signorina,* but what is your name?"

Good manners, I realized, were the first to go in a crisis. "I beg your pardon. My name is Cleo Berry."

Elena gave Mateo one last look before stepping onto the sidewalk. Standing on her tiptoes, Francesca handed me a thin paperback through the window. "Please give this to Mateo when he wakes. It's his favorite."

I looked at the title. *Tarzan and the Jewels of Opar* by Edgar Rice Burroughs.

"I will," I promised, laying the book beside me. From the apartment building, people were pressed up against windows, watching us. I gave Elena and Francesca what I hoped was a reassuring smile before racing down the street.

The Multnomah County Hospital was housed in a graceful three-story Victorian. When I turned onto Hooker Street, I saw two massive tents on the front lawn. Both were round and white, with a pointed roof. They looked like they'd been purchased from a circus.

People poured in and out of the open flaps that served as doors. Patients were being carried in on stretchers. Others were well enough to walk in on their own two feet. No one looked like they had an extra hand to spare, so I dragged Mateo toward one of the tents on my own. It took some doing, and by the time we crossed the lawn, I was breathing hard.

Mateo mumbled beside me. I peered inside the tent, half expecting to see elephants and tigers, or a crowd clutching bags of peanuts and waiting for a show. But no. There were the metal cots, the doctors and nurses, the bad smells, the crying—all of it now familiar.

A man in a white orderly's uniform spotted me hovering. He was short but strong-looking. He lifted Mateo in his arms easily and carried him down an aisle. Relieved, I watched him set the boy on an empty cot. A nurse appeared by my side, her pencil poised above a clipboard. I gave her what little information I could: Mateo's name, address, his father's name. There wasn't much. I hoped I wouldn't have too much trouble locating Nicolo Bassi.

Iron ladders scraped against a steel-hulled ship at the Columbia River Shipbuilding Company, reminding me of fingernails on a blackboard. Assemblymen pounded on metal plates and hollered for bolts. Two dogs barked at a passing produce boat. Horns blasted from the bridge, from the ships in the river, from the trucks rumbling by pulling timber logs, wide as a grown man. Alarming thuds shook the warehouses lining the dock, followed by the *whoooosh* of smoke shooting from chimneys. The drills whirred. The cranes screeched. My ears rang from the sheer force of it all.

I headed toward the dry dock, where a massive cargo vessel stood near completion. A three-story jumble of scaffolding was braced against it, the planks thick with workmen. I hoped someone might be able to point out Nicolo Bassi. The day had warmed slightly. A good thing, as I could not wear my coat. It had been left in the car, along with my shirtwaist, to fester.

I heard a warning shout. A rough hand grabbed my arm and hauled me aside, an instant before a wrench crashed onto the spot where I'd just stood. My heart pounding, I faced the owner of the ham-size hand. I guessed he was old—grandfather old—though the grime on his face made it difficult to tell for certain. His smile was wide and amiable.

"Careful where you stand, miss." He released my arm. "No telling what'll fall out of the sky 'round here." He pointed to the scaffolding, where a man sent an apologetic wave before turning back to his work.

"Thank you," I said.

"No trouble." My rescuer started to walk away.

"Wait!"

He paused and turned back to me, eyebrows raised.

"Do you know where I might find Nicolo Bassi?" I asked. "I was told he works here."

He laughed. "Nicolo? Sure. He's the man who nearly sent you to the hospital." He scratched his chin, adding, "It might be a long while before he comes down, though. The boss wants those plates in by nightfall." With one final smile, he stuck his hands in his pockets and ambled off.

I craned my neck to look at Mr. Bassi, who perched on the highest level of scaffolding. His back was to me, making it impossible to gain his attention. I could not wait here all afternoon, but I hated to leave a message. I doubted he would see it anytime soon.

"Mr. Bassi!" I yelled at the top of my lungs, waving both arms above my head. My voice melted into the din and was lost. Two more attempts failed. How did people work here? I wondered. I could barely hear myself think.

Frustrated, I glanced down and saw the armband. I looked back at Mr. Bassi, considering the distance. Then, raising both pointer fingers, I stuck them inside the corners of my mouth, exactly the way Jack had taught me. A shrill, unladylike whistle emerged. The sound pierced through the wall of noise, causing several men on the scaffolding to glance down.

I ignored them, my attention focused on one man.

When Nicolo Bassi paused, distracted by the whistle, I was ready. He looked down and as soon as our eyes locked, I lifted my arm and pointed directly at the American Red Cross symbol sewn onto the band. I held my breath, hoping he would understand.

He did.

Mr. Bassi's eyes widened. Bemusement gave way to panic. He threw down his wrench, jumped over the two men working beside him, and flung himself onto the ladder resting against the hull. The ladder swayed. Mateo's father clambered down to solid ground faster than I thought possible. Faster, I reckoned, than Tarzan had ever climbed down one of his trees. My nerves frayed as I watched his descent. *Please, Lord,* I prayed. *Please don't let him break his neck.*

With five feet of ladder left, Mr. Bassi jumped onto the dock.

"Who are you?" he demanded, terror lacing his heavily accented English. "*Dov'è la mia famiglia?* Where are my children?"

CHAPTER TEN

Saturday, October 12, 1918

You came back."

"Yes." I hovered in the doorway of the ticket office, riddled with anxiety. Edmund Parrish looked grim, just as he had this morning. Did he always look so serious? Or was he getting ready to share terrible news? I gripped the door frame. "Can you tell me what happened to the family from Caruthers Street?"

The lieutenant stood beside the room's only desk, his white coat replaced with gray trousers and blue shirtsleeves. I'd found him prying open a wooden crate, the word MORPHINE printed along the side. Against the wall, additional crates bore labels ranging from ASPIRIN and DIGITALIS to PAPER CUPS and DISINFECTANT. At the opposite end of the room, through a second door, I could see past the seller's box into the lobby. Hannah was there. She spoke with an older bearded man. His waving hands and panicked expression reminded me of Mr. Bassi.

At my question, the lieutenant set the lid aside and gestured toward the desk chair. "Have a seat," he said. "Relax." He glanced over, and I caught the hint of a smile. "I think you've earned it, after saving three lives today."

I walked toward him on unsteady legs. "You're sure?"

"I wouldn't say that. But we managed to keep some food and water in them. And they don't have pneumonia, which is what we were most worried about." He watched me collapse into the chair. When he continued, his voice was very quiet. "We don't know enough to say how well they'll get along next week. Or next month. But I do know they wouldn't have lasted another night on their own. It was a lucky thing, finding them when you did."

Until that precise moment, I had not realized how tightly I was wound. I pressed both hands to my lips, willing myself not to cry. Not here, in front of a stranger. They were all right for now. What a day this had been. What an awful, wretched, wonderful day.

"You know you don't have to do this."

I looked up and found the lieutenant's eyes on me. This morning I'd been too distracted to notice more than the scar on his hand and the startling green of his eyes. Now I saw that he was tall and lean. Twenty or twenty-one maybe. His hair was dark brown, and rough stubble covered his jaw. Two square-shaped tags hung from his neck; I could just make out his name and rank stamped onto the disks. Like Hannah and Kate and everyone else I'd met today, he looked like he'd passed a hard night. He smelled like soap, though, and I was suddenly conscious of my borrowed blouse, and of the faint, persistent odor of dirty diapers clinging to me.

"I know," I answered, wishing he wasn't standing quite so close.

He glanced through the ticket window. "Hannah's desperate for the help. But I would think very hard before staying on here. There are far more young people in those beds than old ones."

He did not have to tell me that. I had walked down those aisles too. "You're staying," I pointed out. "And you're not very old."

A half smile appeared as he removed glass vials and set them onto the desk. The jars were brown in color and tiny, the length of my thumb. "That's true. But you're what? Fifteen? Sixteen?"

"I am *eighteen*," I said indignantly. Seeing his skepticism, I reluctantly added, "Nearly."

"So you're seventeen." His smile faded. "And you've already helped more than most. There's no shame in walking away. In trying to stay as safe as possible under the circumstances."

I stirred in my chair, suddenly restless. Was there no shame? I didn't think that was true. Not for me at least. My papa couldn't have been saved. Even as young as I'd been, I'd known. From the angle of his neck. From the way he stared at me but did not see.

But maybe, just maybe, my mama would still be alive today had someone thought to look for us. Had someone, anyone, known we needed help.

I touched one of the vials with a fingertip. "There was a story in the newspaper," I said. "About the Red Cross needing volunteers."

"Yes. I saw it."

"I nearly threw it away. But if I had, if I'd stayed home, would someone else have found them in time?"

Something . . . understanding, perhaps, flickered in those green eyes. "I don't know," he admitted.

In the silence, I could hear a raised voice through the glass and Hannah's soothing response.

The lieutenant set the empty crate on the floor. "I beg your pardon." He extended a hand. "I haven't introduced myself. My name is Edmund Parrish."

I grasped his hand, feeling its warmth — feeling also the angry ridged skin beneath my thumb.

We held hands for one heartbeat longer than necessary, then two. Our eyes met. I snatched my hand away, flustered. "Cleo Berry. How do you do?"

Their names were Tess, William, and Abigail Cooke. They slept in a far corner of the hospital floor, at the very edge of the stage. The nurse from this morning, Mrs. Howard, leaned over one cot, the back of her plump hand resting on the infant's forehead. She glanced up as we approached, nodding at Edmund's questioning look. She handed him a chart, surprising me with a quick, tired pat on my cheek. Before I could say a word, she was gone.

While Edmund examined the children's mother, I sat on the edge of the toddler's cot. His face had been washed clean, but he was still very pale. A small arm had escaped from the blanket. I placed one finger on his open palm. It was hot. He didn't move. I leaned over, resting my head lightly against his chest. His heartbeat was quick, fragile, uncertain.

I had asked about their father—was there any trace of him? Edmund said Mr. Briggs, the ambulance driver, had recognized the mother. Her husband was employed by the Southern Pacific Railroad, one of the men who laid the train tracks. Hannah was trying to locate him.

"Cleo," Edmund said, his voice low. I lifted my head. He stood at the foot of the bed, the baby cradled in his arms. Though his smile hid behind his mask, I could see it reflected in his eyes.

Following his gaze, I saw the boy's lashes fluttering. He shifted, the move almost imperceptible, and as I watched, delighted, he closed his fingers over mine in a weak but unmistakable grasp.

My smile faded when I saw Edmund staring past me. I turned. Not ten feet away, a young nurse entered the ward from an adjacent room. Before the door could swing shut behind her, I saw the bodies on the floor. There were three of them, lying side by side, each wrapped head to toe in white sheeting.

The sun had vanished hours before, leaving in its wake a meager sliver of moonlight. Weary, I made my way from our carriage house to the back door, instinct alone preventing me from straying off the path and tumbling into the rhododendrons. I yawned, so wide my jaw cracked the silence.

I let myself in. The kitchen flooded with light. I left my hat on a peg by the door, beside Lucy's tan duster and Mrs. Foster's pink housecoat. My soiled coat and shirtwaist landed in a heap by my feet.

The cozy butter-yellow kitchen was quiet. There was none of the chopping, banging, laughing, and humming I was accustomed to. I unlatched the window over the sink and pushed it open, allowing fresh air to enter.

A small fireplace and two stuffed chairs nestled in a corner, beside the pantry. I fell into a chair, unable to stop thinking of the three bodies back at the Auditorium. I wished I hadn't seen them; I wondered who they were. Who their families were, and if Hannah was responsible for telling them that their loved ones were gone for good. What an awful responsibility that would be.

For the first time I thought, very seriously, of my own death. When would I die? How? From influenza? An automobile accident? Of old age? My parents had passed on well before they should have. What would happen to me?

The telephone ring tore through my macabre thoughts. I nearly jumped out of my skin. A second later I was on my feet and across the room, snatching the receiver from the counter.

"Hello? Hello?"

I heard nothing. Then, "You had better have an excellent reason for answering this telephone, Cleo Marie Berry. Are you trying to give me a seizure?"

"*Jack!* Oh, Jack, are you all right?"

"No." He drew the word out slowly, the way he always did when trying to control his temper. "I am *not* all right. I've spent all day trying to get through to your school on this godforsaken telephone. Only when I did, I received some very interesting news. Quite unexpected."

"Oh."

"Precisely," Jack said. "I was told I would not be able to speak with you, as you'd already left the grounds. Yesterday." Jack allowed his words to resonate. "Your headmistress was under the impression you'd left with me."

I cringed. I knew this had been coming. For the briefest, *briefest* instant, I considered severing the connection and blaming the telephone company. Instead, I said, "I'm sorry, Jack. I didn't think."

"That much is clear," he snapped. "What happened? Didn't you receive my telegram?"

"I did," I confessed. "And I'm sorry I didn't stay at St. Helen's. But I knew you were on your way, and I thought . . . Well, I thought that, under the circumstances, an empty house would be safer than a crowded dormitory." It was not the precise truth. Not even close. But it sounded like it could be.

"Is that so?" A sound emerged—part sigh, part snarl. "Dammit, Cleo, I don't need to be worrying about the both of you right now."

"Both?" For the first time, I realized there was no noise in the background. No chattering, no laughter. Nothing. Usually, Lucy could be heard—a full over-the-shoulder participant in the conversation. I gripped the receiver. "Jack. Where is Lucy?"

"She's resting."

It was dinnertime. And there was something odd about my brother's tone. I raised my voice and repeated, "*Jack.* Where is Lucy?"

"Don't fuss," he said quietly. "She is only resting. Lucy's with child."

"What? Oh. Oh!" My shriek must have ruptured his eardrums. "A baby! But that's lovely! That's wonderful news!"

"Yes." Jack sounded anything but excited. He sounded tired and anxious. "I wouldn't get my hopes up just yet. We've been down this road before. You know it as well as I do."

Just like that, his words deflated me. "Yes," I said, subdued. "Has she seen a doctor? Are there concerns this time?"

"No, Dr. Hess says everything's fine. But he'd rather we not travel for a couple of weeks. What with the influenza and Lucy's history. That's why I called."

Jack's words sank in. They would not be home for weeks. I looked around the silent kitchen.

"I'm seventeen," I said. "Not seven. Remember? Of course you should stay."

"I remember," Jack said, irritated. "Still, I'd feel better knowing you were staying with the Skinners until we return. I'll telephone them myself."

"You can't. They left for Florence on Friday."

There was a pause. "What about the Keatings?"

Mr. and Mrs. Keating had been our parents' good friends. I shook my head, even though he could not see. "I wouldn't feel comfortable asking them. It would be an imposition."

"An imposition? Gerald Keating used to change your diapers. I saw him. Having you stay over for a few weeks can't be as bad as that."

I looked out the window over the sink, staring into nothing. "It's strange here, Jack. Different. And the Keatings have their grandchildren with them. It really would be an imposition."

Another pause. "How bad is it?"

"The hospitals are already crowded," I said. "The Red Cross moved into the Auditorium. It's an emergency hospital now. And they've set up extra tents outside County Hospital."

I heard a long, drawn-out breath. "Christ," he said.

"What about you? How are things there?"

"Bad enough. But we're keeping to our rooms or staying outside. I don't want you to worry. When will Mrs. Foster be home?"

I looked at the note on the counter. Our housekeeper, ever efficient, had left her son's address in Hood River and her return date neatly penciled in just in case we needed it.

"Tuesday," I said.

He sighed. "Do you have enough money? Provisions?"

My eyes traveled to the blue jar on the counter, where Mrs. Foster stored the housekeeping money. There was close to three hundred dollars in there. Almost enough to buy a second Ford if I wanted. "I have both. I had groceries and ice delivered today. And I know where the key to the cash box in your study is. And the numbers to the bank accounts."

"How do you . . . never mind." Jack sounded disgruntled. "I don't want you straying too far from the house. And I don't want you using the streetcars. No good can come from being packed in like a sardine. If you need to get around, take the car."

"The Packard?" I asked, trying to make him laugh.

Jack snorted. "Only when I'm dead. Use the Tin Lizzie. And mind the gasoline levels."

"You don't have to tell me to mind the gasoline levels. I'm not the village idiot."

"Huh" was his reply. There was a long pause. Then, "You're

keeping something from me. I can feel it. There's something rotten in the state of Denmark."

"There's nothing rotten anywhere," I said, the guilt gnawing at me. It was time to change the subject. "Will you have Lucy telephone? When she can?"

"I will. I'm not sure when that will be. These lines are godawful. Send a telegram if you can't get through. And if you need help before Mrs. Foster arrives, promise me you'll go to the Keatings'."

"I promise. And, Jack?"

"Hmm?"

"I am *thrilled to death* about the baby."

"I guess I am too." I could hear the smile in his voice. "Stay safe for me, Cleo. I'll see you in two weeks."

CHAPTER ELEVEN

Sunday, October 13, 1918

I don't mind being alone." I watched Hannah insert a thermometer into a patient's mouth. The girl was younger than me, but not by much, and with her white gown and ashen complexion, she faded right into the sheets. "You're short-handed already."

We were in the orchestra pit, a deep, narrow space in front of the stage that stretched a full fifty feet. Beds crowded together in a single row, leaving just enough room for people—thin people—to squeeze through.

Hannah spared me a glance across the cot. "Short-handed or not, I can't have you roaming about by yourself." She removed the thermometer and studied it. Her brows drew together. She shook the thermometer, waited a tick, and popped it back into the girl's mouth. "Take Sarah with you."

Kate spoke up from the next cot. "Sarah's left, Hannah." She held a cup while her patient, a blond man, drank. "I saw her drive off a half-hour ago. I don't think she'll be back."

Hannah looked at Kate. "Constance?" she asked.

"She's gone too," Kate answered.

Hannah looked at me.

"I can go alone," I insisted.

Hannah sighed. "You can't. I have enough to do without worrying about you being hurt. Or shanghaied and sold to some . . ." She saw my expression and stopped. She pulled the thermometer free. Even with her mask on, I could tell she was unhappy. "No mistake. One hundred and six."

Shocked, I asked, "Is it broken?"

"I wish it were. But that would mean most of them are broken."

The patient lay wretched and shivery on the cot with her eyes half closed. She reminded me a bit of Grace, and I wondered how my friend was faring on the coast. The beaches in Florence would be deserted at this time of year. The sand dunes too. I pictured Grace on the beach, dressed in a heavy sweater and skirt, searching for seashells. I was glad she was far away from here. I looked away from the girl, feeling grateful, and then guilty, that she wasn't someone I knew.

"Hannah," said a deep voice above our heads.

We looked up. It was Edmund. He crouched at the edge of the

pit, wearing a white coat and mask. Seeing me, he tipped his head slightly. "Mornin'."

"Hello." I felt oddly relieved to see him. And Hannah and Kate. Was this how it was to be? Wondering if the person I spoke to one day would be around the next? It was a disconcerting thought. I would try to telephone Lucy and Jack this evening, just to hear their voices.

"How bad is it?" Hannah asked Edmund.

"Bad. We're nearly out of everything. The codeine's almost gone. And we're on our last crate of morphine."

"We'll run out before the next shipment gets here," Hannah said, frustrated. "I've tried calling General Disque to see if he can help, but I can't get past his secretary. That old tyrant. I'll try again."

"I'll do it," Edmund offered.

Hannah looked skeptical. "Do you think it will make a difference?"

He shrugged. "I can try. Old ladies like me."

Hannah snorted. "Then be my guest. Did the numbers come in?"

Edmund nodded. "About eight hundred cases. They're the totals from here, County, St. Vincent's, and Good Sam's. They're estimating the numbers from private residences."

"And the morgue counts?" Hannah asked.

Edmund glanced at me before answering. "Eighteen."

"Total?"

"Yes."

Kate and I looked at each other.

"Eight hundred," Hannah said. "In three days. All right. If you do get through, tell the general we're also running short on aspirin and bandages and . . . well, everything. Just tell him we need everything. Right away."

"I will." He looked over at Kate. "Waverley telephoned. She'll be by after her shift to take you home."

"Thanks, Edmund."

He stood and, with one last glance in my direction, strode off. I watched him go. When I turned back, Kate was eyeing me with a funny look on her face.

Hannah planted both hands on her hips. "What were we talking about?"

"Being shanghaied," I said.

"Ah. Let's see. Marion and Charlotte are both on the east side today. Paul is in St. John's. Who's left?" She surveyed the room. I looked too, but from where we stood, all I saw were the undersides of cots.

Kate cleared her throat.

Hannah continued. "I can't spare Rose. She's helping Mrs. Howard with the laundry . . ."

Kate coughed. She looked exasperated, but Hannah appeared oblivious.

"Well, why don't you head to the ticket office," Hannah said to me. "There's a fresh list on the desk."

Kate's face fell. I sent her a sympathetic look and turned to go.

"And, Cleo?" Hannah said.

"Yes?"

"Be careful today." A small smile appeared on her face. "And take Kate with you."

The rain had stopped, leaving the air smelling fresh and clean. As Kate and I traipsed down Lovejoy Street, with its pretty houses and manicured lawns, she closed her eyes and breathed in deep, like a newly released prisoner.

I smiled. We had spent an uneventful hour together. I had told her about Jack and Lucy in San Francisco. And I'd learned a great deal about Katherine Bennett as well. Like me, she was seventeen and would graduate from high school in the spring. Her family lived on the outskirts of town, where the Bennetts had owned a dairy farm for generations. Kate's mother had been a nurse until she'd married. Several of her older sisters were nurses or training to become nurses, and though Kate didn't say so outright, I imagined she would follow in their footsteps. I liked her very much. She was smart and practical, and she did not faint at the sight of blood. In times like these, they were good qualities to have in a friend.

"It's nice to escape the hospital for a little while," Kate said.

"I don't think I'll take fresh air for granted again. God bless Edmund."

Surprised, I asked, "What do you mean?"

Kate glanced at me sideways, enough for me to see the humor in her eyes. "He told Hannah that sending you out alone was irresponsible. He said there were all kinds of lunatics out there, and what was she thinking? I heard them in the kitchen last night after you left."

My eyes narrowed. "Edmund called Hannah irresponsible? Because of me?"

"Well, he phrased it differently. But yes. And he didn't sound too worried about anyone else being sent out alone. Just you." Her smile widened. "You must have made quite an impression."

Kate was enjoying herself, but I didn't find her words the least bit funny. Did he think I needed looking after? What did he know about anything? I was embarrassed that he'd spoken to Hannah. Had forced her hand. Especially when the hospital was so short-staffed.

I tried not to let my annoyance show. "Hannah called him 'lieutenant,'" I said. "Why isn't he at one of the camps with the other soldiers?"

Kate's smile disappeared. "He's already been to training camp. And to France. My sister Waverley knows him. The medical and nursing schools are right next to each other. She said he'd just started classes last year when he had to ship out. But he was hurt, and they sent him home. I don't think he's been back very long."

"Was he sent home because of his hand?" I asked, even though that didn't make sense. Men were coming home missing entire arms and legs. Edmund's hand looked dreadful, but it still worked. I'd seen him carry babies and pry open crates. I didn't think the army would send him home for that kind of injury. They were desperate for men.

Kate shook her head. "I think it's more than his hand. He was in a hospital for a good long time. I asked Waverley about it, but she told me to stick to my own business." She frowned. "It looks terrible, doesn't it? Like someone used his hand for target practice."

I winced, imagining all sorts of horrible scenarios that would send Edmund to a hospital for "a good long time."

We stepped aside as three boys raced by on their bicycles, whooping and hollering, before disappearing around the corner.

We walked on.

"It must be lonely living in that house all by yourself," Kate said. "I can't imagine it. We have an extra bed, now that Etta's moved out. You'll have to put up with Ruby's snoring, but you're welcome to stay with us. My mama won't mind at all."

I stopped, surprised. It was a completely unexpected and generous offer. And from a near stranger during times like these. "I really am fine," I said. "Our housekeeper will be home in a few days. But it's very kind of you to . . ." I trailed off, looking over Kate's shoulder.

Puzzled, Kate turned. A two-story home stood before us, painted blue with white shutters. I followed her eyes past the picket fence, down the stone path, up the shallow porch steps, to the small piece of white fabric attached to the front door.

Kate wrapped both arms around herself. "Already," she said softly.

It was considered tradition to hang a piece of wool crepe on the door to announce a death in the family. White crepe meant someone young had passed on. Black represented middle age. And gray was meant for the very old. Coming across such a sight used to be a rarity. I had an awful feeling this would be the first of many.

We watched the narrow strip of fabric flutter in the wind. A memory rose, of Jack, white-faced, climbing our porch steps and yanking the black ribbon from our door. I brushed the image aside and tucked my arm into Kate's.

"Let's go," I said. "I don't think they need us here."

We rounded the corner. The three boys we had seen earlier stood just ahead of us, their bicycles left on the sidewalk in a tangle of metal and rubber. They were about ten, fair-haired and freckled, dressed in matching denim overalls. Try as I might, I could not tell them apart. Kate and I looked at each other, diverted. Triplets!

The brothers did not see us, so preoccupied were they with the low stone wall in front of them. Curious, I turned to see what had captured their attention.

"Oh!" I said.

Kate's hand flew to her mouth.

The boys jumped, turning in unison to look at us with identical blue eyes. One of them recovered first.

"We didn't do it," he piped up, pointing at the wall. "We found it like this. Just now. It wasn't us." The other two shook their heads vigorously, their eyes wide and earnest.

Along the wall, someone had painted the word *kaiserite* in red. It was a vicious slur reserved for war protesters and deserters. And German immigrants. Each letter measured at least three feet and had been allowed to drip, so that it resembled a great big bloody wound.

"We know you didn't." Kate gave the boys a reassuring look. "Do you know who lives here?" Behind the wall stood an elegant gray house with black shutters. Two stone urns flanked the front door.

A second boy spoke up. "The Kruegers, miss. Mr. Krueger, Mrs. Krueger, and their son, Daniel Krueger. Our pa said Daniel Krueger left Camp Lewis last week."

The third boy chimed in. "Just upped and ran away, even though the army said he couldn't."

A deserter. A Kaiserite. So that was it.

"Are the Kruegers home now?" I asked.

They shook their heads. "They have the influenza," said the first brother. "The ambulance came yesterday. We heard the sirens and everything."

"We can't just leave this here with them sick," Kate said in a low voice.

"No." I looked at the wall, calculating the amount of hard scrubbing it would take to get all the paint off. "But we're hardly dressed for *that*, Kate."

She eyed my red coat, then looked down at her own blue skirt and jacket. "You're right."

She gave the boys a considering look. They were thin but sturdy. Their denim overalls and long sleeves looked one step away from the rag pile. She reached into her canvas bag and rifled around until she found a small purse. Snapping it open, she pulled out a single dollar bill. It was crumpled and sad-looking.

She grimaced. "Do you have any money, Cleo?"

"Sure." I reached into my own purse and pulled out the handful of dollar bills I'd taken from the jar on my kitchen counter. I gave it to Kate. She counted, gave me back half, and held up the money. The boys straightened. Kate fanned the bills out until their eyes looked ready to pop right out of their heads.

I smiled.

"Well, boys," Kate said. "School's out and there's nothing to do. How would you like to earn some money?"

The three brothers looked at one another, partaking in some sort of silent communication that included quick headshakes, pursed lips, and crossed arms. Finally, the first brother spoke up, sounding far more calculating than any ten-year-old had the right to sound. "How much money?"

The house was unlike any other on the street. Tall and narrow, it was painted forest green, with a gray scallop-edged roof and wraparound porch. A lovely home, but it was the windows that captured the eye. The windows that gave one pause. Curved and graceful, they had been shaped to resemble giant keyholes.

"Look at this house, Cleo!" Kate said. "It's beautiful! It . . . Why are you smiling like that?"

I gestured toward the house as we walked up the path. "Do you really like it?"

"I adore it. It looks like a dollhouse. Why?"

"It was one of the first houses my brother built. He used to bring me here after school sometimes, during construction."

Kate's eyes widened. "Is that true?"

I nodded. "Look at the owl," I said, pointing.

We climbed the steps. A carved wooden owl perched on the railing. It was ten inches high, round and wise as it looked out onto the street. Kate *ooh*ed and *aah*ed when she realized the porch rail and the owl were one piece, carved from a single length of wood.

"I've never seen anything like it." She bent to take a closer look. "Your brother must have a romantic soul."

I made a face. "I wouldn't go that far. And please don't ever tell him that."

Kate laughed. She knocked on the door. When no one answered, she shrugged. "I'll check the back."

Kate disappeared around the side of the house. Within minutes she reappeared, unconcerned. "Nothing. I looked in the kitchen window. Everything looks fine. They must be out."

I couldn't help picturing Tess Cooke in her bedroom. Unable to call for help. Too far gone to realize she even needed it.

"Let's ask the neighbors," I said. "Just in case."

"Sure."

We retraced our steps down the path.

"My brother Gabriel loves to build things," Kate said. "He would spend all day with his blocks if my mama—"

A thud, faint but unmistakable, sounded behind us. We spun on our heels.

"What was that?" My eyes darted around the immaculate yard.

"I don't know. It sounded like . . ." Kate's hand clamped around my arm. She pointed up at the house. "Look!"

On the second floor, a crack had appeared in one of the keyhole windows. Even as we watched, it grew, spreading across the glass like a spider's web. I met Kate's shocked stare, then raced back up the steps and tried the door.

"It's locked!" I said.

Kate ran toward the side of the house. I sprinted after her. On the back porch, an assortment of blue flowerpots crowded near the door. Kate was already on her knees, lifting one pot after another.

"This door is locked too," she said without looking up. I dropped to my knees and started pushing aside pots. One tub was bigger than the others and flowerless, but still filled with dirt. I shoved it aside and saw a brass key.

I held up the key, triumphant. "Found it!"

We scrambled to our feet. I fumbled with the lock. It finally turned. We ran through the kitchen, down the hall, and up a curved staircase. The air was scented with lemon polish and candle wax. Portraits flashed by on the walls. I caught a glimpse of dour men and women dressed in old-fashioned clothing.

At the top of the landing, four rooms branched off. Kate rushed directly to the far end of the hall. I followed, glancing through open doorways as I passed. The first room, a bath, was empty. Across from the bath, a tiny bedroom was unoccupied. Feeble sunlight streamed through the window onto a cradle and a stuffed blue chair. A nursery.

In the third room, a baseball bat stood in the corner beside a desk. The bed was unmade, the patchwork quilt kicked aside. A lone white sock languished on the wood floor. On the nightstand was an old Kodak camera and an empty glass.

"Cleo!" Kate shouted.

I rushed to the last room. A man and woman lay on the bed beneath a pile of bedcovers. The man might have been in his thirties, with damp red hair plastered against his skull. His eyes were closed. The woman was awake, her hair also red, but wild and curly. She shivered as Kate lifted her head and held a glass of water to her lips. The smell of urine, sharp and pungent, saturated the air.

I looked toward the cracked window and saw an apple on the floor beneath it. The woman had thrown it, I realized, to catch our attention. I wondered how she had found the strength.

"Slowly," Kate said, as the woman gulped the water and choked. "There's plenty." She looked over at me, pale and tense. "We can't carry them. He's far too heavy, and she's in a family way."

For the first time, I noticed the large bump beneath the covers. "I'll be right back," I said. I ran down the stairs, searching, relieved when I came across a study. A telephone sat on the desk. I lifted the receiver. There was a crackling noise over the line. A woman's voice said, "Only essential telephone calls are permitted at this time. What is the nature of your call?"

"I need an ambulance!" I tried to stay calm, but my voice still sounded breathless and panicky. "I have two patients with influenza. One is with child. Please—"

The operator interrupted, sounding frazzled. "Your address?"

I gave it. "Will you be terribly long? The woman is—"

"Help will be sent directly." And with that, the phone went silent.

"Aargh!" Vexed, I dropped the receiver and ran up the stairs.

"They're on their way," I said, at Kate's questioning look. We both knew that could mean anything. Kate pressed a cloth against the man's forehead. The woman had fallen asleep, and the sound of labored breathing filled the room. I unlatched the damaged window, careful as I pushed it open. As an afterthought, I pulled on my mask.

"I wonder how long they've been like this," I said.

"Long enough." Kate pointed her chin at the night table, where a newspaper lay beside the water glass. "It's yesterday's paper."

"I should wait outside. I don't want them to miss the house."

Kate nodded. "I'll be fine."

The ambulance arrived forty minutes later. Kate and I stood on the sidewalk as the stretcher-bearers loaded the man onto the truck. He was still unconscious. The woman grasped my hand as she was carried past, and would not let go. I bent my head to her ear.

"You're both being taken to the Auditorium." I tried to reassure her. "To the hospital. You're safe now."

But the woman only gripped my hand tighter. "Jamie," she whispered. "Please." She dropped my hand and disappeared into the truck. A moment later, the ambulance sped off.

"That was terrifying." Kate watched as the truck grew smaller in the distance. "I just want to sit down and cry."

I was only half listening. I turned to look up at the cracked window.

"Cleo?"

I dashed back into the house and up the stairs, entering the bedroom where I'd seen the baseball bat and camera. Draped over a chair was a navy school jacket. I picked it up and turned it over. My scalp prickled.

Footsteps sounded in the hall.

"For heaven's sake, Cleo." Kate walked in, aggrieved. "What is it?"

I held up the jacket so she could see the name neatly stitched onto the inside of the collar. Jamison Jones.

"Kate," I said. "Where's the boy?"

We searched the house from top to bottom. We looked under beds and inside armoires. Kate ran outside to check the shed. I peeked into the attic, earning nothing but a face full of cobwebs for my trouble.

In the study — a room filled with heavy wood and dark leather — Kate and I examined a framed photograph on the mantel. Mrs. Jones was seated. She wore an enormous feathered hat. Mr. Jones stood behind her, gruff and serious, along with a skinny teenage boy who looked just like his father.

"Did she actually say he was missing?" Kate asked.

I shook my head. "She just said his name. And she said please."

"Please what?"

"I don't know," I said, frustrated.

Kate was quiet for a moment. "She was sick, Cleo. Maybe she didn't know what she was saying. He could be with relatives. I'm sure he's fine."

Her words made sense. More sense than my own doubt—that tiny niggling feeling that refused to leave me alone. I tried one last thing. Jack had built this house, after all, and he had learned from Papa. I walked over to the glass-fronted bookcase. Standing on tiptoe, I carefully felt along the top edge.

Kate came to stand beside me. Her expression made it clear she was beginning to think I was touched in the head. "What are you doing?"

I felt along the sides, brows knit in concentration. "There's a room hidden behind my brother's study. The only way to get in is by pressing a button on the bookcase."

"A secret room?"

I nodded.

Kate searched the opposite edge of the shelf. "What do you have in it? Gold? Jewels?" She sounded intrigued.

I smiled. "Mostly just drawings and plans." And crate upon crate of illegal whiskey, but I kept that to myself. Kate looked disappointed. Finally, I stepped back, feeling foolish. "You're right. There's no one here."

Kate laid a comforting hand on my arm. "It's good he's not

here. It means he's safe somewhere else. Let's go out through the back. We can lock up and leave the key where we found it."

I agreed. In the hall, a grandfather clock stood directly below the staircase. I'd been so distracted earlier that I'd overlooked it. It was made of pale blond wood. A curving hourglass figure gave it a feminine appearance. An owl perched on a narrow ledge just below the clock's face. A carved wooden owl, just like the one on the porch.

Without thinking, I reached for the bird and tried to shove it forward, then back. When it didn't budge, I twisted it, like a door-knob.

"What . . . ?" Kate began.

We heard a loud click.

The clock wheeled slowly to the side before shuddering to a stop. A doorway was revealed. An odd smell tickled my nose. I was reminded, strangely, of the chemistry lab at school. A muted red light appeared, and I heard Kate gasp behind me.

It was a darkroom.

Photographs were strewn about the tiny floor space, along with several cameras and upended shallow trays. Lying in the midst of it all was a teenage boy. He was curled into a ball, and he was shivering, his lips so cracked they'd started to bleed. He looked exactly like his father.

Jamison Jones.

CHAPTER TWELVE

Sunday, October 13, 1918

It poured all afternoon. Raindrops, sharp as pebbles, whipped at our faces, and the wind tried its best to send our skirts right over our heads. Kate and I scurried back to the Auditorium hours earlier than we'd intended. Hannah wasted no time putting us to work. After we'd dried off, she'd given us each a white apron to protect our clothing. Kate was sent to help in the kitchen. I was to go upstairs to the new ward for women and children.

Downstairs, the orchestra floor had grown crowded. So had the assembly rooms. Doctors and nurses slept in cramped dressing areas behind the stage. Many of them had not left the Auditorium in days. Despite the shortage in staff, Hannah had managed to move all the women and children to the second floor.

I stood in the doorway and looked around. A dance troupe

must have used the room as practice space. It was bright and airy with wooden floors, scarred and scratched. Barres were pushed up against a wall covered in mirrors. A single pair of pink ballet slippers hung from the chandelier, dangling by a length of satin ribbon.

This ward had fewer beds. I counted sixty or so cots. Nurses and volunteers went about their business. Dr. McAbee, whom I'd met yesterday, was off in a corner. He was a large man, gruff but kind, with a white mustache and eyes that protruded slightly — reminding me a bit of a walrus.

Edmund was halfway down one aisle. Seeing him, I remembered Kate's words. I squared my shoulders and headed his way, ready to tell him, politely, to mind his own business. But I faltered when I came across Mrs. Jones. Her pregnancy looked even more pronounced under a thin blanket. She slept soundly, having been told that Jamison was downstairs with his father. But Hannah had kept the seriousness of their condition to herself; both Mr. Jones and his son were doing badly.

I lingered by the foot of the bed, wondering at the unfairness of it. Kate and I had found them alive. We'd sent them here. Yet it still might not be enough to save them.

Beside Jamison's mother, a woman coughed and coughed and coughed. I left Mrs. Jones and gave her neighbor some water, which didn't help. Mrs. Howard was over at the next cot, sponging down a little girl who'd soiled herself.

There was a small medicine bottle on the shared nightstand. "Should I give her the codeine?" I asked the nurse, holding up the bottle.

Mrs. Howard glanced over, harassed. "Yes. Just a teaspoon. Mark it on her chart."

I did. Then I continued down the aisle, tensing when I saw Edmund leaning over William Cooke's bed. My carefully prepared lecture flew from my head.

The boy lay on his side. Asleep or drugged—I didn't know which. "Is he worse?" I asked. I glanced at the nearby beds and squeezed Edmund's arm. "Where's the baby?"

The children's mother, Tess Cooke, slept in her bed. The cot beside her had the tiniest rumple in the center. It was empty.

Edmund was masked. But his eyes were smiling, despite the nails I dug into his arm. "She's right there." He inclined his head toward the next aisle. "With Mrs. Clement."

Mrs. Clement was another volunteer, a widow whose youngest son had been killed in Europe. She was cradling Abby's head against her shoulder with one hand as she walked down the aisle, bouncing her gently.

"And William is a little worse," Edmund continued. "But this I can fix. Are you squeamish?"

I dropped his arm. "Why?" There were some questions you never wanted to be asked in an emergency hospital.

"Sit there, on the bed." When I did, Edmund lifted William so his head rested across my lap. "I need you to hold his head here and here." He demonstrated, cupping one hand along the back of William's head, the other against his chin. "He needs to be kept perfectly still."

William whimpered in his sleep, a pitiful sound. Apprehensive, I did as I was told. The boy's hair was a pure black, like mine, and his soft curls wove their way through my fingers. While I held the child's head, Edmund pulled up a chair and sat before us. His hair was damp, slicked back from his forehead. I wondered if he had gone home to bathe and to have a few hours of sleep in his own bed. Or if he'd just used the showers by the dressing rooms — the ones normally reserved for performers. I saw my own tiredness reflected in his eyes. His face, handsome and serious, looked the tiniest bit thinner than it had yesterday. It made me wonder what he'd looked like before. Before the Spanish influenza, before the war.

Edmund peered into William's ear. A tray had been placed within reach on a small rolling cart. On it was a white porcelain bowl, a stack of gauze pads, and a collection of needles lined up in a row. There were clear glass bottles, five of them, the writing on the labels scrawled and illegible. Edmund reached for an instrument I did not recognize. It looked like a spoon, only the scoop part was much narrower, elongated. I watched as he used it to scrape dark yellow wax from William's ear. He cleaned the spoon with the gauze, then continued the removal. He scraped and scooped, scooped and scraped. I looked at the wax sticking to the cotton. There was a disgusting amount of it. I would never look at a spoonful of honey the same way again.

Not wanting to disturb Edmund's concentration, but too anxious to stay silent any longer, I asked, "What happened?"

Edmund set the spoon in the bowl with a small clatter. "He woke up earlier complaining of an earache. It's common enough with flu, but with Spanish flu it's worse. He has otitis media."

I frowned. "Is that Latin?"

Edmund kept his gaze fixed on the child's ear. "Hmm? Sorry, yes. He has a bulging eardrum," he clarified. "His drum membrane is about to rupture." He selected a needle from the tray.

Uneasy, I looked from the needle to William's vulnerable, exposed ear, guessing Edmund's intent but unwilling to believe it. My voice was faint. "What are you going to do?"

"I need to remove the extra fluid. It'll relieve some of the pressure. Hold him still, Cleo." And then in a move that nearly stopped my heart, he inserted the needle, thin and wicked-looking, directly into William's ear canal.

There were several ways to control one's urge to vomit. In just the last day, I had learned this. Breathing through your mouth was one. The other was to concentrate on a single thing with all your might. To focus so entirely that everything else receded into the background. For this gruesome occasion, I chose William's mother.

Someone had washed her hair. It lay pleated in two braids over her shoulders, ending around her elbows. She lay on her back. With a start, I realized she was awake. We were in the center of the room, and the chandelier hung directly above us. Tess Cooke stared at the crystals glinting in the light, blinking in wonder, like an infant in a cradle.

She must have felt my stare, because she turned her head with such painful slowness that my head throbbed in sympathy. Her eyes were light blue, shot through with tiny red veins. She might have been pretty once. It was impossible to tell.

Where was Mr. Cooke? All we knew was that the railroad company he worked for had been notified. That didn't tell us anything. It could be days, weeks even, before he was tracked down by telephone. I hoped he'd return soon. His wife didn't look well at all. I was glad that she couldn't see past Edmund to her son, who lay unmoving with a needle in his ear. I smiled at her, the only comfort I could offer, and watched her eyes close.

Edmund continued to work away. Curious despite myself, I glanced down. He'd replaced the needle with a small suction instrument, which was just now removing a thick, reddish-yellow substance. My stomach rolled, though this time I was unable to look away. It was both fascinating and revolting to watch. William whimpered.

"Nearly done, William," I whispered. "What a brave boy you are. We're nearly done."

Mrs. Clement approached with Abigail. She stopped when she saw what Edmund was up to, turned on her heel, and marched off in the opposite direction, a protective hand cupping Abby's head.

My curiosity shifted from bulging eardrums to Edmund Parrish. He looked perfectly calm and capable. But I knew he couldn't have had very much medical school training. Not with being shipped off to war. Or recovering from his injuries.

"How many of these have you done?" I asked.

Still working away at William's ear, Edmund asked, "Ever?"

"Yes."

"This is my second."

"What?" My hold on William tightened.

"Dr. McAbee showed me how to do the first one," he said, and I could tell he was fighting a smile. "You just prick and scoop. Don't worry. I won't let anything happen to your buddy here." He glanced over in Mrs. Jones's direction. "Busy morning?"

And I remembered, suddenly, why I'd sought him out. "Yes." I added, "I took Kate with me. Just like you wanted."

He paused, the suction instrument hovering over William's ear. "You don't sound happy about it. What's wrong with Kate?"

"There's nothing wrong with her," I said, exasperated. "And you know it. Hannah couldn't spare her. You shouldn't have said anything."

He didn't bother to deny it. "Hannah's responsible for everyone under her care," he said evenly. "That includes you."

"I could have gone on my own. I'm not a simpleton, Edmund."

His green eyes narrowed. "No. But you're a pretty girl, knocking on doors, in all kinds of neighborhoods. All alone. What happens if you knock on the wrong one?"

I opened my mouth, closed it. Grisly scenarios danced around in my imagination. "That's hardly cheery," I finally said.

He shrugged. "It wasn't meant to be. And you can go ahead and be mad. I'd do it again."

Edmund went back to work, looking stubborn and unrepentant. I scowled at the top of his head. But as I saw firsthand how gentle he was with William, my annoyance began to fade. After several minutes, I couldn't take his silence any longer.

"I'm not mad," I said grudgingly.

"Good." He dropped the instrument into the bowl. Taping a thick bandage over the boy's ear, he said, "Let's turn him over. It'll drain anything I've missed, and I can have a look at his other ear."

We shifted William. I held him still while Edmund began the process all over again.

"Have you always wanted to be a doctor?" I asked, watching him remove the needle from William's ear.

"Since I was ten."

There was the oddest inflection to his voice. I heard it, and I told myself that I should practice what I preach and stick to my own business.

"Why?" I asked.

Edmund exchanged the needle for the suction instrument. "My mother died of tuberculosis when I was ten." His gaze flicked to mine, then dropped. "I want to know why."

The words *I'm sorry* lingered on the tip of my tongue. But I knew what it was to be young and to lose your mother. And I couldn't remember the number of times I'd been told *I'm sorry.* Or told my loss was part of *God's will* or *God's plan.* Well-intentioned words, every one of them. But they'd never made me feel better. Not one single bit.

"What did you want to be before you were ten?" I asked.

Edmund looked surprised. His eyes crinkled at the corners. "A judge, I guess. Like my father. And a cowboy. I'd forgotten." He cleaned off the instrument with a fresh square of gauze, then asked, "What about you?"

I had not meant to say it, but it came out anyway. "I haven't the slightest idea."

He looked amused. "I wouldn't worry about it. You're only eighteen . . . nearly. Sometimes you need to go out in the world and live a little first."

I stared at him, hearing the echo of my brother's voice.

Edmund attached a bandage to William's other ear before glancing up. "What is it?"

I was saved from answering by William, who woke and started to cry. His wails frightened a nearby baby, who began howling. The wailing set off a vicious cycle; before long, the room had erupted in an earsplitting cacophony of weeping children. Edmund and I exchanged a panicked glance. He fussed over William while I hurried across the way toward another toddler. Mrs. Howard exclaimed, *"Lord, what now!"* I scooped up a little girl. And after that, there wasn't any time left over to think.

CHAPTER THIRTEEN

Monday, October 14, 1918

I'm sorry, Lucy."

"We do not set these rules in place to torture you, darling." My sister-in-law's voice was faint and tinny-sounding over the telephone line. "They are for your own good. When I give you specific instructions, I do not expect to be ignored. Is that clear?"

"Yes, ma'am," I said, subdued. Pushing the tangled mess of hair from my face, I looked around the upstairs hall. A tiny yellow bird emerged from the wall clock and sung a gentle morning cuckoo. I counted six chirps and stifled a groan. Six o'clock in the morning. Lucy had always been an early riser.

Lucy continued. "Well, what's done is done. Jackson says you have provisions, and I'm sure Mrs. Foster will order more when she returns. But other than deliveries, not a soul enters that house. Is that understood?"

"Yes." I paused. "Are you well? The baby . . . ?"

Lucy's voice softened. "You sound like your brother. This feels different, Cleo, and—"

The telephone operator interrupted. "At this time, we are permitting emergency calls only." Her tone was firm. "It has been determined that this conversation does not meet our emergency standards."

"I beg your pardon?" Lucy said.

At the same time, I said, "Wait!"

The operator ended the call. I tried to reconnect, but the line remained silent. I looked at the telephone, wide awake now and infuriated. I did not have the chance to tell Lucy how happy I was about the baby. I did not even have time to say goodbye.

I was in the ticket lobby, waiting for Kate, when I felt it: a faint rumbling beneath my feet, growing stronger and stronger with each passing second. Others in the room felt it too. It was eight in the morning. A handful of people were already gathered in the waiting area, hoping to learn how well, or how badly, their loved ones had fared overnight.

Hannah was conversing quietly with an older couple who looked as though they hadn't slept in a week. She stopped and glanced over at me. "What on earth is that?" she asked.

I lifted both hands, just as lost. Hannah said something to the couple, before heading for the outer doors with me close on her heels. Standing at the top of the steps, we peered down Third Street.

At first we saw nothing but a wet sidewalk and an overcast sky. Then a large truck appeared around the corner, followed by a second one, and a third, fourth, and fifth. Five trucks in all pulled to a stop, taking up the entire length of the Auditorium. Painted along the sides in bold black letters were the words U.S. ARMY.

Soldiers spilled out of the trucks like worker ants, unloading crates and disassembled cots onto the sidewalk. Hannah looked astonished. They had clearly not been expected.

A familiar figure jumped from the back of the first truck. "Hannah, look," I said.

Hannah followed my line of sight. A rueful smile appeared. "I might have known," she said, as Edmund strode toward us, along with another soldier.

It gave me a jolt to see him dressed as he was, in olive drabs, with a smart cap and brown boots that laced clear up to his knees. What was it about a military uniform, I wondered, that had girls making cow eyes even at the homely boys and turned someone who already looked like Edmund into . . . I fumbled for my mask before realizing I'd left it in the car. I could have used a mask right now. I was sure everything I thought and felt was written plain on my face.

We met them halfway down the staircase. At the last moment, my boot came down on a slick step. Edmund's hand shot out. He grabbed my elbow, steadying me. Without acknowledging my clumsiness or even saying hello, he pulled me close enough so that our arms touched before dropping his hand. He looked unruffled, as though being pressed against his side was the most natural place for me to be.

Hannah's eyebrows arched upward. I stared straight ahead, painfully self-conscious, but she let the moment pass without comment. "All this," she said to Edmund, "because old ladies like you?"

Edmund grinned, turning toward the soldier who'd accompanied him. I eyed the blond stranger, wary. Edmund was tall. This man was taller. And fearsome-looking, with wide, powerful shoulders, a hawk nose, and stern features. He looked like he could take on the entire German army on his own.

"Hannah, this is Sergeant Simon LaBouef with the Army Spruce Division," Edmund said. "Sergeant, this is Mrs. Hannah Flynn. She's in charge of all Red Cross operations here at the Auditorium. And Miss Cleo Berry, also with the Red Cross."

Sergeant LaBouef stepped forward. After a brief nod to me, he said, "Mrs. Flynn, General Disque wishes to convey his deep regret that he was unable to meet with you in person." He gestured toward the trucks. "Everything you requested is here. Beds, as well as bandages, masks, pneumonia jackets, codeine —"

"Morphine?" Hannah asked.

"Yes, ma'am. Lieutenant Parrish says you're short on staff?"

"Very."

The sergeant glanced behind him. "Twenty men will stay, myself included. With your permission, we'll set up barracks here for as long as necessary. You can put us to work as you see fit."

Hannah pressed a hand to her cheek, looking slightly overwhelmed. "Thank you, Sergeant. I assure you I will. This is very unexpected."

"The general was unaware of your identity when you telephoned, ma'am," he said. "Lieutenant Parrish was kind enough to clear up the confusion." Sergeant LaBouef clasped both hands behind his back, his demeanor growing even more formal. "I had the honor of knowing Captain Flynn personally. Your husband was a brave man and an excellent soldier. You have my assurance that any request you have will be addressed immediately. The United States Army is deeply sorry for your loss."

I watched Hannah as the sergeant spoke. And saw, then, the grief that flashed across her face before vanishing.

"Thank you, Sergeant. Edmund," Hannah said. She drew herself up. "Now, where should we put your men? I think the stage would be best. It's not ideal, but it's where we have room. You'll have some privacy, at least, with the curtains drawn. And we can move some of these cots to the second floor."

Hannah and the sergeant wandered off discussing logistics,

while soldiers hustled up the steps carrying crates and beds. People poured out of the Auditorium to see what the fuss was about. Kate spotted me and headed my way. She stopped when she saw Edmund, smiled, and walked in the opposite direction. I stepped away hastily so that a decent amount of space lay between us.

"When did he die?" I asked, watching Hannah inspect one of the crates.

"Captain Flynn? In the spring," Edmund answered. "He came down with influenza in France. It turned into pneumonia."

Captain Flynn had died of influenza. And now Hannah was working herself into exhaustion, trying to save every flu patient in her care. It made a terrible, wretched sort of sense.

"Do they have children?" I asked.

He nodded. "A boy. Matthew is seven. I think he's staying with his grandmother until this is all over." He tipped his head toward the last truck, which the soldiers had not yet unloaded. "Give me a hand?" he asked.

"Sure."

Edmund hoisted me into the back of the truck. Wooden crates of varying sizes filled the cavernous space, along with metal headboards, footboards, and side rails. I lifted one of the smaller crates. Edmund grabbed one of the large ones. We passed them down to the soldiers who waited at the edge of the truck.

"Can I ask you something?" Edmund held a footboard and headboard in each hand.

"Yes," I said.

"Are your parents liberals?"

The unexpectedness of the question made me laugh. "Liberals? Why?"

He smiled back. "Well, most girls aren't even allowed to answer their front doors anymore. But you're driving around, visiting every sick house in the city. Your parents sound more liberal than most. Like Kate's."

I passed a side rail down to a freckled soldier who looked younger than I did. "I don't know if they were or not. They died a long time ago." I saw his grimace, waved off his apology. "I live with my brother, Jack. He is the opposite of a liberal."

He looked surprised. "Your brother's Jackson Berry?"

"Do you know him?"

"I've heard of him. Is he your guardian?"

I nodded. "And his wife, Lucy. They'll be home from San Francisco in a few weeks." I wished my words back as soon as I spoke them. Why oh why did I say that? Now he would wonder . . .

"Where are you staying while they're gone? With other family?"

I hesitated. "There's just the three of us."

Edmund glanced at me, and I looked away. "So you're living with friends?"

Very carefully, I handed down a headboard. "No."

Turning back, I inspected the crates, taking my time deciding which one to lift next. The seconds ticked by in silence. I heard a solid thump as he set his own crate down a few feet away. I hoped it wasn't filled with morphine.

"You're living by yourself?" Edmund sounded incredulous. "There's no one else with you?"

It was beginning to feel uncomfortably like the Spanish Inquisition. Irritation sparked. I was not a child, and I did not need Edmund worrying about me. Again. "It's only been for a few days. Our housekeeper will be home tomorrow." It took some effort, but I kept my tone reasonable, hoping that would be the end of it.

Edmund refused to let it go.

His green eyes narrowed, showing the first signs of temper. "Cleo, what if you'd fallen ill before then? Hannah doesn't check on volunteers who don't show up. She'd never get anything else done."

"I've been very careful," I said, defensive. "I always wear my mask when I'm with patients. I've washed my hands so much they're raw." I held them, palms up, so he could see. "And I sleep with my windows open. I'll be fine."

Edmund looked unimpressed by my diligence. "I wouldn't put much faith in that mask if I were you."

"What do you mean?" I'd been wearing that rotten itchy mask for days. I saw now that he had not bothered to tie one around his neck. How come? Did he know something I didn't?

"I mean you might as well try to keep the dust out with chicken wire." He leaned against a stack of crates and folded his arms. "I was at St. Vincent's last night. There are two nurses, one chaplain, and two doctors lying in those cots. All of them wore masks. All of them followed the rules. And all of them are sick. And not one of them is over thirty years old."

I gripped the sides of a crate but did not lift it. In my head, Lucy's soft, lilting voice reminded me that I did not get into arguments with boys I hardly knew. Especially not in the back of trucks.

"You're trying to frighten me," I said.

He muttered something rude under his breath. "I am trying to show you how careless you've been. You—" He looked down, startled by the finger I'd poked into his chest.

"*You* live in a flu hospital!" I snapped, pointing toward the Auditorium. "You eat here, breathe here, *sleep* here, and then lecture me on staying safe. You are a black pot, Edmund Parrish!"

"Maybe so." His voice, though soft, was just as angry. "But if I were sick, everyone here would know it. I am accounted for, every hour of the day. And if I'm not where I'm supposed to be, someone comes looking. It is common sense, Cleo." He took a deep breath, fighting for patience, which only made me madder. "You could be dead in your empty house, and no one would know it. What do you think that would do to your family? To anyone who cares about you?"

There was an awful truth to his words. I knew it, but just then

I would rather have jumped off the Hawthorne Bridge than admit it. We glared at each other. I looked away first.

"I have to go," I mumbled. "Kate's waiting." Seeing me at the edge of the truck, the freckled soldier smiled and offered up his hand. I reached for it.

"Cleo," Edmund said.

There was an apology in his tone. It stopped me. I looked over my shoulder. Edmund stood in the center of the truck, hands shoved deep in his pockets, his face half lost in the shadows.

"Maybe I was trying to scare you," he admitted. "A little. I'm sorry. It's just . . . It bothers me that no one is watching out for you." Silently, the soldier glanced back and forth between us, his eyebrows raised right up to his hairline.

It bothered him. Well, it bothered me too.

"I am not your responsibility," I said. Without another word, I grabbed the soldier's hand and jumped onto the street. I marched off, wondering what in God's name had just happened.

This is a terrible idea."

"Five minutes," Kate insisted. "We'll buy our lunch and leave in five minutes. Look, we can eat over there." She pointed down the street, toward the entrance to a square.

"I don't know . . ." I cast a dubious glance at our surroundings. Thousands of circulars had been distributed, warning everyone to keep away from crowded places. Was no one reading them? Or were they just ignoring the flyers, as we were about to do? There was no place in the city more crowded than this.

Kate's sigh lasted a full three seconds. "Cleo, I'm famished. It's five minutes. Come on!" She grabbed my hand, and, against my better judgment, I allowed myself to be pulled into the throng.

The Carroll Public Market stretched along Yamhill Street for three long blocks. Each morning, hundreds of vendors converged, hawking everything from eggs to cream to freshly slaughtered meats. A family sold jars of warm, golden honey, while one mustachioed vendor shouted, "Oranges! Sweet oranges!" The heady aroma of frying potatoes filled the air. Housewives arrived on streetcars, baskets swinging from their arms, taking advantage of the break in the weather. The women rubbed elbows with businessmen and laborers and vagrants, each haggling for the lowest prices on the choicest offerings.

We passed a stand displaying crates of juicy Spitzenberg apples. A short, stocky man stood beside it, polishing the bright red fruit with his apron. He held the apple up to us, a persuasive smile on his face. I smiled and shook my head, then glanced at the clock tower. It was one o'clock. We had spent the morning visiting one rooming house after another. I was very hungry, which always made me snappish, and my mood soured even further every time I thought about Edmund Parrish.

Which was often.

In the hours since I'd seen him, my indignation had shifted to a deep embarrassment. Because I'd come to accept that, to Edmund, I was my own sort of unattended case. Not sick or helpless, but on my own. Without anyone knowing where I was or whether I made it home safely. He'd only been concerned, and I'd stormed off in a huff—after jabbing him in the chest. I relived our conversation over and over again, wincing every time.

"My brother Charlie says that if you scowl like that, and someone slaps you on the back, your face will stay that way forever," Kate said.

"Very funny," I said.

Kate tucked her arm into mine. "Don't be mad at him for keeps, Cleo. He means well."

"He hardly knows me."

"Why does that matter? *I* hardly know you," she pointed out. "But I still worry." She stopped in front of a cheese vendor and pointed to a small orange wheel. "How much?" she asked.

While Kate haggled, I wandered over to a neighboring stand that sold fresh bread. It was run by a stooped elderly woman. A worn red kerchief covered her hair. I dropped coins into her outstretched palm and tucked a long, crispy loaf into my empty bag. It extended a foot behind me. This part of Yamhill was closed to automobiles, and as I rejoined Kate, we made our way down the center of the street toward the square.

"Pardon me," said a voice behind us.

We turned. A young man stood with a rolled-up newspaper

in one hand. He had a rugged, muscular look about him: dark curly hair and eyebrows so thick they nearly met above his nose. He wore a black topcoat and yellow scarf, overdressed for the weather. Pinpricks of sweat beaded his forehead.

"I beg your pardon," he repeated, tipping his hat and offering a friendly smile. "I've just arrived in town. I wonder if you could tell me where I might find the Dekum Building?"

"Certainly." I pointed down the street, past the hotel and courthouse. "It's a few blocks that way. You'll want to turn right on Washington Street."

"The Dekum will be several blocks down," Kate added. "It's difficult to miss."

The stranger glanced down the street, before he said, "I'm obliged to you both. Good day, ladies." After one final cheerful smile, he tipped his hat again and strode off. We watched as he made his way around a tired-looking woman pushing a stroller. Six well-dressed children — all blond, all masked — trailed behind her in a single row like ducklings. They ranged in age from two to ten. The younger children were amusing themselves with a song. As they passed, I heard:

Tramp, tramp, tramp, the boys are marching
I spy Kaiser at the door
And we'll get a lemon pie and we'll squash it in his eye
And there won't be any Kaiser anymore.

Which reminded me . . . I turned to Kate. "How many brothers and sisters do you have?" I asked.

"Thirteen."

I stopped dead in my tracks. Fourteen children in total! I couldn't imagine a worse fate. I struggled to clear my expression, hoping Kate had not seen my horror.

Too late.

Kate looked at me with good humor. "Believe me, I know. Robert and Charlie are my older brothers. Then there's Waverley, Etta, Ruby, me, Amelia, Celeste, Annamae, Michael, James, Dexter, Jonathan, and Gabriel. Gabriel is two."

"That's . . . that's lovely," I lied.

Kate laughed. We continued on our way. She gave me a sideways glance. "There are ways to prevent babies. Did you know that?"

My head whipped around. It was the very last thing I expected to hear. "How would I know that?" I asked, keeping my voice low as we were jostled on both sides. "How do *you* know that?"

Kate grinned. "Waverley used to bring all kinds of interesting things home from the hospital. I found a birth-control booklet once, written by some nurse in New York City. It's fascinating. I'll bring it tomorrow so you can see."

"What does it say?" I asked, curious despite myself. I realized I had never heard the words "birth control" spoken out loud before. Not even by Margaret. Certainly not by Lucy.

Kate thought for a moment. "Well, she recommends condoms, but you have to make sure they don't break." She laughed at my expression before continuing. "Then there's the sponge, and the douche, and Beecham's Pills. And women in France use the pessary all the time. It's supposed to be very efficient."

"What is it?"

"It's a rubber—"

A woman screamed. Startled, I looked around. A crowd had gathered on the sidewalk just outside the Portland Hotel. Several pointed to a prone form lying on the ground. It was a person. A person. And no one was trying to help.

Kate and I exchanged a frantic glance and sprinted over.

"Cleo," Kate puffed beside me, sounding scared. "The scarf. I think it's the same man."

It was. We knelt on either side of him. He lay face-down, his hat crushed beneath one shoulder. We turned him over. His eyes were closed. In the minutes since we had last spoken, blood had appeared on his face, streaming from his nose and soaking his yellow scarf.

"Oh!" I cried.

Kate lifted the man's head off the sidewalk so it rested against her skirt. Blood dribbled onto her.

Around us, I heard the whispers of *influenza* and *plague* and *la grippe*. Someone said the man didn't have a prayer. A woman on a bicycle swerved around us without stopping. I looked into the crowd, saw the anxiety and the fear. Everyone took care not to come too close.

I jumped to my feet. "I'll get the car," I said.

Kate's eyes were wide with fright. "Hurry," she said, but I needed no further urging.

I ran.

The car was parked three blocks away. I returned within minutes, pressing the horn so the other drivers would clear out of my way. The crowd had thinned, though people continued to walk by with their eyes averted. Kate looked at me and shook her head. Stunned, I dropped to my knees and checked his pulse. One thumb pressed lightly against his inner wrist, the way I'd seen Hannah and Edmund do it. I felt nothing.

He had been alive and well minutes ago, asking for directions.

The man's newspaper had fallen to the ground. It was a special edition I had not yet seen. The headline read INFLUENZA WANES IN PORTLAND, SERIOUS SPREAD UNLIKELY.

PART TWO

What's true of all the evils in the world is true of plague as well.
It helps men to rise above themselves.

—Albert Camus, *The Plague*

PART TWO

CHAPTER FOURTEEN

Monday, October 14, 1918

Kate slammed the car door shut and ran up the Auditorium steps. I followed at a snail's pace, watching as she vanished inside. My feet were heavy, sluggish. I tried to make sense of what had just happened but could not.

Not everyone had forsaken us on that busy downtown sidewalk. Help had arrived in the form of a man and woman rushing across the street toward us. They were an older couple, round and gray-haired, with white aprons. They had stopped in front of us.

"Well, hell," the old man had said. He stared down at the stranger, whose head still rested on Kate's lap.

The woman's plump hands flew to her cheeks. "Is he . . . ?"

When Kate didn't answer, I struggled to my feet. "He . . . we saw him in the market. Just now. He was fine and then . . ." The old man knelt and checked for a pulse. He sat back on his haunches and sighed. I continued. "We're with the Red ... the Red ..." I gestured helplessly toward Kate's Red Cross band. Toward mine. I could not string an entire sentence together, could not work through my muddled thoughts. I tried again. "If you could please help us lift him into the car, we can take him with us. To ... to the morgue. Is that where we're supposed to take him?"

Kate looked at me. The color had leached from her face, and her brown eyes were enormous. She shook her head. "Cleo, no. Please."

I didn't want to take him with us either. I looked at my car, recoiling at the thought of him lying in the seat behind me. But what else could we do?

The woman pressed a hand against an ample bosom. "You girls won't take him to the morgue! The idea! Franklin?"

The old man lurched to his feet. "No need to bother with an ambulance now," he said. "I'll get the truck. Emmett and I will take him." He waved over another man who watched from across the street. The sign behind him read ROYAL BAKERY.

Numb, I waited as a truck was brought around and the body of the young man placed into the back. The woman untied her apron and laid it across his face. I placed his hat beside him. I wondered who he was. Who his parents were. Kate stared at the ground. Onlookers watched from a distance. After the two men drove off, the woman invited us back to her shop to sit for a spell. But neither Kate nor I wanted to linger. We thanked her, then drove to the Auditorium in silence.

Hannah burst through the doors, stopping when she saw me standing halfway up the steps. She took in my appearance from head to toe, and relief flooded her face.

"What on earth happened?" She came down to meet me. "Kate's off crying in the stairwell. She's covered in blood. *Who* is bleeding?" She stopped when she saw my chin tremble. "Cleo," she said, her voice softer. "What happened?"

I told her, trying my best to keep the tears at bay, but as I finished reciting my awful tale, the tears spilled over. Hannah pulled me close, and I wept like a child in her arms. Above my head, I heard her murmur, "How much more of this can we take?"

Someone had wedged the basement door open with a stack of old sheet music. Faded, yellow, bound together with thin brown string. A piano sounded in the distance, telling me I was in the right place. After I'd spent several hours in the kitchen helping Mr. Malette, the cook, I'd gone in search of Kate. Hannah had told me to look downstairs. *Go to the basement,* she'd said, *and follow the music.*

I stepped over the bundle and found myself in a dimly lit corridor with a low ceiling. I passed one closed door after another, the music growing louder with each step. Goose bumps appeared on my arms. It was colder down here than in the wards. I came across another door propped open with more sheet music. I peeked in and found myself looking around in wonder.

Several floors above, nurses calmed the ill and comforted their families. Doctors injected morphine and closed the eyes of the dead. But here, in this windowless room, was a symbol of the Auditorium's original purpose.

Pushed against the nearest wall was a tangle of musical instruments. Violins, violas, cellos, and flutes. Clarinets, bassoons, and piccolos. A French horn and a trombone. Some were locked in their cases; others were not. A thin layer of dust gathered atop a harp and a bass drum. I remembered Hannah mentioning that a symphony was to have performed the night the Auditorium was turned into a hospital. Were the musicians too frightened to return? Lining the remaining walls were stacks of chairs, four high, and row upon row of music stands.

In the center of the room, isolated and grand, was a piano.

Kate's long, elegant fingers flew across the ivory keys, so fast they blurred. Her eyes were closed. I recognized Beethoven's Sonata No. 8, his *Pathétique,* and was astounded. It was a melancholy, brilliant, difficult piece. One I'd practiced countless times, one I could never quite master. Kate played it effortlessly.

I sidled in and stood just inside the door. To my relief, I saw that Kate had exchanged her bloodstained clothing for a fresh shirtwaist and skirt. When the piece ended and the music faded to silence, she opened her eyes. I saw they were red and swollen.

"Did Hannah send you with the hook?" she asked. "I know I'm not supposed to be down here."

I walked toward her. "There's no hook. I wanted to see how you were. I can take you home if you like."

"Thanks, Cleo. But Waverley will come."

I gave her arm a nudge, and she made room for me on the bench. Neither of us was in a hurry to say anything. In the quiet that followed, I realized, a little shamefully, that I had made an assumption about my friend, based on what little I knew of her family.

I gave her a sidelong glance. "You don't want to be a nurse, do you?"

A small smile appeared. "I've never wanted to be one," Kate said. "When I was in grade school, my great-aunt Beatrice used to take me to these shows: symphonies, operas, the ballet. Once a month, just the two of us. My brothers and sisters thought she was strange, because she never married and she liked to travel all by herself. But I adored her." She ran a finger lightly over the keys. "When Aunt Bea died, she left me her piano. And enough money for lessons. We never could have afforded it on our own. Sometimes I wonder how different my life would be if she hadn't."

"I've never heard Beethoven played like that before," I said. "Truly."

Bright spots of color appeared on her cheeks. "It's sweet of you to say, Cleo."

"Well, I mean it. What will you do? Study at a conservatory?"

She nodded. "Next summer. I've been offered early enrollment at a school in New York."

"But that's wonderful! Which one?"

"The Institute of Musical Art. Have you heard of it?"

I stared at her, open-mouthed. Had I heard of it? "Kate, that is the best music school in the country."

"It is." Kate shook her head, as though she still did not quite believe it. "And best of all, they're offering me a full scholarship. I haven't told anyone except my family. The letter came last week, before—" She broke off. "It came before. Do you know his name?"

Abrupt as it was, I was ready for her question. "Henry Thomas," I said. "Hannah thought we would want to know. She sent Sergeant Briggs to the morgue. They found his wallet and notified his uncle."

"Who . . . ?"

"Otto Thomas. He owns a printing office in the Dekum Building."

Kate looked up at that. The Dekum Building. "Where was he from? Didn't he say he was new to the city?"

I nodded. "He came in on the morning train from Astoria. His parents are on the way." I felt sick inside as I said the words. "Hannah says it's not uncommon for someone to die so quickly from influenza." When Kate didn't respond, I added, lamely, "There are plenty of cases in Philadelphia and Boston."

Kate snorted. "That doesn't make it any less awful, does it? You saw how young he was. He could have been you. He could have been me."

I didn't know what to say to that, so I said nothing.

"Have you ever seen anyone die? Before today?" Kate asked.

"Yes."

Kate waited for me to elaborate. The silence stretched.

"I haven't," Kate finally said. "My brothers and sisters and I are hardly ever sick. But now Robert and Charlie are in France, and there's the flu. I try to be brave. Like my sisters. Especially Waverley. And like you. But I'm so scared my luck is going to run out."

Tears sprang to my eyes at her words. I thought of Edmund, warning me that I was being careless. I blinked them back, then wrapped an arm around Kate's shoulders. Our heads touched. "No one will blame you for not coming back. Not Hannah. Not anyone."

Kate swiped at a tear. "But you'll stay."

"Just for a few more days."

Kate turned to study me. "I won't pry, Cleo. But maybe one day you'll tell me why. When everyone else is running away."

I dropped my arm. "Why don't you play something?" I suggested. "Hannah knows where we are if she needs us."

"Oh. Well . . ."

I nudged her shoulder. "Just one? It might be my last chance to listen for free."

Kate's laugh was more of a hiccup. She relented. After taking a deep breath, she squared her shoulders. She brushed at her skirt. She pulled herself together. Then, in a dark corner of the hospital, in the lingering footsteps of death, in the company of drums, Kate played Bach.

I moved away, so her arms would have room to fly.

CHAPTER FIFTEEN

Monday, October 14, 1918

The sun was a distant memory by the time I descended the Auditorium steps. Torch lights blazed along the front of the cream-colored brick, banishing the darkness as though anticipating a crowd of opening-night revelers. But the sidewalks and streets were nearly empty. Only two of us braved the cold, crisp outdoors on this night.

The man stood on the sidewalk beside a gleaming automobile. He was dressed in a chauffeur's uniform. A wicker hamper hung from one gloved hand. He watched my approach before lifting his cap, revealing a shiny bald head.

"Good evening, miss." His voice was low and pleasant, the deepest I'd ever heard.

"Good evening." I eyed the hamper. "I'm very sorry, but

visitors aren't permitted inside the wards. Would you like me to deliver that for you?"

Relief flickered across his face. "If it's not too great an imposition." He held out the hamper. "This is for Lieutenant Edmund Parrish."

Oh.

I had not spoken to Edmund since the morning. In the truck. After returning to the Auditorium, Kate and I had stayed close for the rest of the day, on Hannah's orders, but Edmund had been sent to St. Vincent's to help with some catastrophe there. I'd caught a glimpse of him an hour ago heading backstage, and though I knew full well the polite thing to do would be to seek him out and set things right, I'd been rather hoping to avoid him. Forever, if possible.

It was not meant to be. The stranger was offering the hamper, and I had no choice but to take it. It was heavier than it looked. A delicious aroma escaped from the lid, reminding me that I had not eaten since breakfast.

"Is there a message?" I asked.

"Just that Lafayette sends his regards. And if the lieutenant is able, his father would be pleased to dine with him at home on Sunday."

Although it was phrased as an invitation—a gracious one—I had a feeling Edmund had better not miss Sunday dinner if he knew what was good for him.

"I'll tell him, Mr. Lafayette. Good evening."

"Just Lafayette, miss." He lifted his hat once more. "Good evening."

Edmund was not in the main ward or in either of the adjoining assembly rooms. Hannah thought she had last seen him in the kitchen, which also functioned as a temporary dining hall. Several soldiers congregated at one of the tables. They pushed their dinner around their plates with little enthusiasm. One soldier muttered something about gas bombs and monkey meat. Edmund was not among them. A search of the ticket lobby, the box office, the smoking room, and both coatrooms also proved fruitless.

The carpentry area was a cavernous space located beneath the stage. Hearing voices, I poked my head in. Two volunteers were stuffing large sacks with straw. Both were older: the widow Mrs. Clement and Mrs. Pitt, a retired nurse who'd recently moved from Seattle to live with her daughter. I knew the bags they filled would be used for fresh bedding. Propped against the wall behind them were several large pieces of scenery. The wooden boards were at least ten feet high and eight feet wide, painted in shades of swirling blue to resemble waves.

Mrs. Pitt spotted me first. "I thought you would be long gone by now." She peered over her spectacles. "After the day you've had."

"I'm on my way, Mrs. Pitt. I just wanted to give Lieutenant Parrish this hamper." I held the basket up. "Have you seen him?"

Both women looked at the hamper, then at me.

"You've brought Edmund Parrish his dinner?" Mrs. Clement asked.

I felt my face turn red. "No! No, a man came with—"

"You don't have to explain anything to us, dear," Mrs. Pitt interrupted. She raised an eyebrow toward Mrs. Clement. "I think it's lovely."

"But—"

"The lieutenant was on the stage an hour ago," Mrs. Clement said. "With the sergeant. Have a nice dinner, Cleo."

"Thank you, but you don't . . ." I started to explain about the basket, then gave up. I left the carpentry room to the sound of laughter.

Frustrated, I wandered upstairs onto the stage.

"Are you looking for someone, Miss Berry?"

At the front of the stage, the fair-haired Sergeant LaBouef sat on a cot with a black boot in one hand and a stained polishing rag in the other. He set the items aside and stood. He must have been four or five inches over six feet. Though he padded across the stage barefoot, I realized he wore far more clothes than the men around him. I stared at the assortment of bare chests and hairy legs lounging about on metal cots.

A dozen pairs of eyes stared back.

"I beg your pardon," I stammered. My eyes darted up to focus on the lighting and cables dangling from the ceiling. I tried not to think of how red my face must be; even my ears felt hot. "I'm looking for Edmund . . . for Lieutenant Parrish."

A chorus of good-natured boos and groans erupted from the soldiers.

"What does the lieutenant have that I don't have?"

My gaze dropped. The question had come from the skinny, freckled soldier who'd helped me from the truck this morning. His question was met with an unflattering litany.

"Money."

"Class."

"Deodorant."

"Knock it off," Sergeant LaBouef said mildly. He looked at me. "The lieutenant's bunking down in one of the dressing rooms." He eyed the hamper. "Do you need a hand with that?"

I stepped back and shook my head, careful to keep my eyes trained on the sergeant. I gave him a weak smile. "Thank you. I'm fine." Spinning on my heels, I left the stage with my dignity in tatters.

The door to the first dressing room stood wide open. Great bearlike snores emerged, loud enough to raise the rafters. I peeked in. Lights blazed around a mirror set above a dressing table. The tabletop suggested someone had left in a hurry. A jar of face powder lay overturned, its contents spilled across the surface.

Pots of rouge and lipstick were scattered about, alongside bottles of perfume and at least a dozen cosmetic brushes. A towering white wig, the kind Marie Antoinette would have worn, perched atop a bust.

Across from the dressing table, a snoring figure occupied every inch of cot space and more. His stomach rolled off the sides. Although the top half of his face was hidden behind a black sleeping mask, I had no difficulty recognizing Dr. McAbee.

I crept by the room, frustration turning into annoyance. My shoulder ached. Where was Edmund?

The second dressing room door stood ajar, revealing a shadowed, silent interior. I stuck my head in. A long, lean figure lay on a cot, naked to his waist. Edmund. At my entrance, he flung an arm up to shield his eyes from the light pouring in behind me.

"I'm so sorry!" Grabbing the door, I started to pull it closed.

"Cleo, wait."

Reluctantly, I waited just outside, listening to the rustling within. Wishing I had left Mr. Lafayette to deliver his own basket. I leaned against the wall, realizing I'd seen more naked male chests in the past five minutes than I had in my lifetime.

The door swung open. Edmund stood there in dark trousers, trying to shove an arm through a white shirt. My breath caught. Before he pulled the edges of the cloth closed, I glimpsed the puckered tissue marring his torso. The wounds were identical to the one on his hand. One disfigured the skin below his left shoulder; another formed an ugly tattoo above his navel. Two more spoiled the flesh just beneath his heart. I was right. He'd been shot. My stomach churned. Four bullet wounds, plus the one on his hand. How was he still standing?

"Hey."

I blinked, blushing when I realized Edmund was watching me stare at his now-covered chest. His eyes were bleary and unfocused, and his hair stood above his head in wild brown tufts. Despite what I'd just seen, I could not help but smile.

"I'm very sorry," I repeated, holding out the hamper. "This is for you. I didn't want it to get cold."

Edmund took the basket. I shook my arm out, relieved to finally be rid of it.

He peered in, flabbergasted. "Have you brought me dinner?" His voice was deeper than usual and scratchy from sleep.

I shook my head. "Mr. Lafayette was outside. He sends his regards. And your father wants you home for dinner on Sunday."

Edmund smiled at this. He brought the hamper close to his nose and sniffed. "Ah, God bless Mrs. O'Reilly." He looked up. "Thanks for this. Have you eaten?"

"I couldn't eat your dinner." Just then, my stomach betrayed me and rumbled. In the quiet, it sounded like a building had collapsed. I wondered if it was possible to die of embarrassment.

Edmund studied me, unsmiling. "This morning, I wasn't very . . . that is . . ." He trailed off, then sighed. "I'm a chump, Cleo."

"Yes."

His lips twitched, but his eyes were serious. "I didn't mean to scare you. I wouldn't have you upset for anything. I am sorry."

I scuffed the tip of my boot against the floor. "I'm sorry I poked you."

This time the smile reached his eyes. "Well, there was no harm done. So . . . truce?"

"Truce."

Satisfied, he looked at the basket. "Then you'll have dinner with me? Mrs. O'Reilly is my father's cook. She always makes enough for an infantry." He tipped the hamper so I could see it was filled with neatly wrapped packages.

"If you're sure."

"Great. I . . ." He ran a hand through his hair and winced, probably realizing what a sight he was. His rueful gaze met mine.

I laughed.

"Shhh!" The surly command came from the first dressing room. I stared at Edmund, wide-eyed.

Edmund leaned close. "I'll meet you on the upper balcony. Give me a few minutes?"

I agreed and retraced my steps, careful to tread lightly as I passed Dr. McAbee's door.

Our seats were so high up, we nearly touched the rafters. Edmund and I unpacked the hamper, setting the packages on a wide ledge that ran across the front of the upper balcony. We took care not to set the food or china too close to the edge, not wanting anything to go tumbling onto the lower balcony. Or, worse, onto the sea of patients sleeping below.

I pulled my mask down. Unbuttoning my coat, I laid it across one of the red leather opera chairs. Then I surveyed the bounty before me in awe. I had expected a few sandwiches. Maybe some cookies. Instead, there was thinly sliced pheasant, generous servings of mashed potatoes and asparagus, and pears that smelled as if they'd been baked in maple syrup and cloves. A feast.

"What does Mrs. O'Reilly cook on special occasions?" I asked.

Edmund smiled. His hair had been ruthlessly tamed by a comb, though he hadn't bothered with a lab coat. "She knows what they serve in the kitchens here. I think she feels sorry for me."

He offered me a delicate white plate rimmed in silver, the kind usually reserved for Thanksgiving and Christmas dinners. Then, waiting until I'd filled it, he heaped a small mountain of food onto his own plate and settled beside me.

Mrs. O'Reilly was an artist. Edmund must have thought so too, because we both tucked in, neither of us bothering with conversation. I set my empty plate on the ledge within minutes. Edmund reached for seconds.

When he finally came up for air, Edmund set his plate aside, then fell back into his chair with a sigh. His shirtsleeves were rolled up just beneath his elbows. I studied his wristwatch with interest. Sergeant LaBouef had worn one too, I recalled, but prior to that, the only wristwatches I'd seen had been worn by women. Slim, delicate pieces. Edmund's watch looked nothing like those. The band was much wider, for one, and the silver looked battered. This watch had undergone some rough use.

"Is that comfortable?" I asked, indicating his watch.

"It's taken some getting used to," he said, a little self-conscious. "I still reach for my pocket watch sometimes. But it's more convenient." He indicated my plate. "Feel better?"

"Yes. Thank you. I haven't eaten since breakfast."

He frowned. "I heard about what happened at the market," he said quietly. "I'm sorry for it, Cleo."

I took my time before responding. "Hannah said he was only twenty-one."

"I heard, yes."

"How old are you, Edmund?"

The silence went on for so long I thought he would not answer. "I'm twenty-one . . . Cleo . . ."

I looked away. "Kate won't be back tomorrow."

"No? It's hard to blame her."

"She said something earlier, about running out of luck. About tempting fate. And I wonder now if that's true. Like you, for example."

He glanced over, surprised. "What about me?"

"Well, Kate said you were hurt in France. You haven't been out of the hospital very long, have you?" I stopped, realizing I was being rude. "I don't mean to pry. It's just that I saw your other bullet wounds backstage, and I—"

"I wasn't shot, Cleo."

I looked at his hand, mystified. What else could it be? "What do you mean?"

He glanced at his scar, frowning. "I was on patrol one day. I had an unlucky encounter with a German cat stabber." He shrugged. "So they sent me home."

"A cat stabber?"

"A bayonet."

I was rendered speechless. Sickened, I imagined Edmund curled up on the ground, trying to fend off a long, thin blade. Failing five times. "This is what I'm trying to say!" I sputtered. "You were stabbed by a . . . a bayonet. And now you're working in a flu hospital. You're pushing your luck. You shouldn't be here."

He smiled then. I bristled. Of course he'd have a laugh at my expense while I tried to have a deep philosophical discussion.

He held up one hand in peace. "I'm not laughing at you. But you're starting to sound like me." He gave me a pointed look. "*You* shouldn't be here."

I looked away. I did not discuss my parents with anyone. Not with strangers, not with friends. But suddenly, it was very important that he understand. "There's an old road near Zigzag," I said. "It runs by a ravine with a giant fir tree growing from it. Do you know it?"

He straightened. Alerted by my tone, or by my question, I didn't know which. "Yes."

I focused on the stage curtain. "When I was six, my parents attended a party given by one of my father's clients. I was usually left at home with our housekeeper, but these clients had small children. I was allowed to dine with Alice and Peter in their nursery. I remember feeling very grown-up."

I watched as the curtain shifted to and fro, nudged by unseen soldiers. "The rain started soon after we left. It was the kind of rain that came at you sideways and left the roads great big muddy rivers. Our driver, Mr. Logan, lost control of the horses."

I felt Edmund's stillness beside me.

"One moment I was falling asleep against my mother's side, and the next our carriage had plunged off the road, down the ravine, and into that old tree. My father and Mr. Logan were killed instantly. And the horses. I was unhurt but for a few scratches."

I had not spoken of the accident in years. And then only to Jack and Lucy. The images were washed-out, like an old sepia photograph, but the sounds refused to dim. I remembered my father's shout and the frantic neighing of the horses.

I remembered my mother screaming.

"It was very late when we set off. No one saw the accident."

A silence fell and lingered.

"How long were you in the carriage?" Edmund asked quietly. "Before someone found you?"

I looked at him. "No one found me. I waited all night. Until my mother . . . until she passed on. It was morning, and the rain had finally stopped. I climbed out of the carriage, out of the ravine, and walked until I found help."

I had walked for miles, keeping Mount Hood in my sight. Numb with grief and shock. Shivering with cold. A farmhouse had appeared around a bend. A giant, grizzled man had answered my knock with a pipe cradled in one hand. He had stared at my bloodstained dress, at the cuts on my face, before turning and yelling, *"Martha!"*

My breath hitched at the memory. I didn't realize how hard I gripped the armrest until Edmund covered my hand with his. Silver glinted off his wrist, and his skin was warm and callused. He said nothing, only laced his fingers through mine, carefully tracing the side of my palm with his thumb. The gentle rhythm of it steadied me, until, gradually, I felt the tightness in my chest ease. I tilted my head back to look at him.

"You wonder why I stay," I said. "Sometimes I wonder too. But I hate to think of a child, of anyone really, lying somewhere sick and scared, waiting for help that does not come."

CHAPTER SIXTEEN

Tuesday, October 15, 1918

The morning dawned damp and gloomy. Green, gray, wet. But as I stopped the car outside the Auditorium, I felt my spirits lift. Like the first hint of sun after a storm.

Kate stood at the top of the steps, dressed for warmth in a blue coat and hat. A black umbrella kept the raindrops at bay. Her Red Cross bag rested against her boots. She spotted me and clambered down the stairs. The passenger door swung open.

"Morning, Cleo."

"Hi."

She climbed in and tossed her bag and umbrella onto the rear seat. I eyed the paper sack in her hand.

"Blueberry?" I asked.

"Cinnamon," she said, apologetic. She tipped the bag so I could see the cinnamon cakes. "It was all they had." She tugged her gloves free and removed one cake, showering the seat with sugar and crumbs. "I saw Hannah. She wants us to stop off at the library first. One of the librarians is sick. And then we're to spend the morning in St. John's. I have the addresses." She set the paper sack beside me.

"Thank you." I paused. "Kate, I'm glad you're here."

Kate looked rueful. "Well, I'm hardly Florence Nightingale. My mother won't allow us to sit at home and do nothing. So. I could spend the day with you. I could mind my brothers and sisters all day. Or I could help my father and Ruby with the cows at the dairy. You win, Cleo."

I laughed.

"This is for you." Kate tugged something from her coat pocket. She held it up. I thought it was one of our influenza brochures, a little rumpled, but when I looked at the cover, it read: *FAMILY LIMITATION* BY MARGARET SANGER.

"Who is she?" I asked.

"The lady who wrote about birth control. Remember? I found Waverley's old copy."

I snatched the pamphlet and shoved it deep into my coat pocket.

Kate laughed. "Oh, and Hannah wants to see you before you leave today. I'm to tell you that you are absolutely not to go home without checking with her. Once in the morning and once at night."

I glanced over, perplexed. "Why?"

Kate shrugged. "I guess she found out your family was stuck in San Francisco." She saw my look. "I didn't tell her! I didn't breathe a word."

"Sorry."

It bothers me that no one is watching out for you.

I shook my head, exasperation mingling with affection. He was consistent at least. I was glad Kate didn't notice the color rising to my cheeks. Smiling a little, I looked once over my shoulder and pulled the car into the street.

Why would the library still be open?" I asked. "Who needs a book that badly?"

"Lots of people, I guess. Look," Kate said.

We were standing on the sidewalk at the bottom of the public library steps. A trio had just emerged from the three-story Georgian building: two men and a woman, their arms full of books. To the right of the doors, an old man sat on a bench with a book held close to his nose. A small dog slept by his feet.

I shook my head, baffled. The schools were closed. The theaters, bowling alleys, and churches too. So why was the library open? Some of the new city rules just didn't make a whole lot of sense. Some did. Such as the telephone company asking everyone to keep their calls to a minimum. There was an operator shortage, and the lines were bogged down. I understood that. Even though it meant the only sure way to contact Jack and Lucy was to send a letter. Or, God forbid, to stand in line at the Western Union Telegraph office. I'd driven past the office yesterday. It was downtown, by the Skidmore Fountain. And the line of people — miserable, resigned-looking people — was so long, it had wrapped clear around the block.

But I wondered how telling us we couldn't buy candy at certain times of the day was helpful. Because that was another rule. The sale of candy, ice cream, and tobacco before nine in the morning and after three thirty in the afternoon was strictly prohibited.

Then there was the Meier & Frank Department Store, which placed an advertisement in the newspaper, asking customers not to come in unless absolutely necessary. Why bother? Why not just close the store down entirely? Who had emergency clothing needs anyway? Although, now that I thought about it, maybe I did. Or would soon. The pile of laundry in the washroom had grown beastly high. Thank goodness Mrs. Foster was coming home today. I'd had quite enough of living on my own.

Kate and I walked into the library, past the marble columns and up the main staircase. Our footsteps echoed in the quiet. At the top of the stairs, in the rotunda, I whispered, "Where are we supposed to go?"

"Hannah said to look for Mrs. MacMillan," Kate whispered back. "She's expecting us."

Everyone knew Mrs. MacMillan. She was the head librarian,

and had been forever. When I was younger, she never minded when I forgot myself sometimes and spoke too loudly. Unlike Miss Tarbell, the assistant librarian, who was always scolding and shushing.

Just off the rotunda was the reading room. We peeked in. Arched windows ran along an entire wall, beginning six feet off the ground and soaring high above toward the carved plaster ceiling. Bookshelves filled the space beside card catalogs and oak tables.

A massive four-sided circulation desk dominated the center of the room. Mrs. MacMillan stood behind it. She was small and thin, birdlike, and wore a high-necked gray dress the same shade as her hair, which was pulled back in a braided roll. I guessed she was in her sixties, but I couldn't be sure. Jack swore she'd been in her sixties when he was a kid. Miss Tarbell, wide-hipped and sturdy, sat at the back of the desk area. A great stack of books teetered beside her.

People waited in front of the desk. Every one of them was masked. But rather than stand directly behind one another as was the usual practice, the men and women in line were spaced at least five feet apart. I imagined I could step between any pair, arms spread wide, and spin around without knocking into anyone. I glanced about. There was something else strange about the room. What was it? It dawned on me. All the chairs had been removed. A sign on the wall ordered NO LOITERING.

At the head of the line, a boy several years younger than me stood before Mrs. MacMillan with his head hanging low.

"You may insist all you please, Mr. Dosch, but late is late. And a fine is a fine." Resignation seeped through the librarian's mask, suggesting this was not the first time she had articulated these words. She looked over and spotted us. Her gaze fell on our armbands. She said something to Miss Tarbell, who lumbered over to take her place, then she hurried toward us.

"Goodness!" she said in a loud whisper, glancing back and forth between us. "Cleo. Katherine. Hannah Flynn sent you?"

"Yes, ma'am," Kate and I said together.

"I see." Mrs. MacMillan wrung her hands. The look in her eyes asked why Hannah was sending her schoolchildren.

Kate tried to reassure her. "The car is right outside, Mrs. Mac-Millan. Hannah said she was still able to walk?"

"Yes. Yes. Cora is the new children's librarian. She was coughing when she arrived. A terrible sound. And her right ear is bleeding. There's no one at home to care for her." She gave us another dubious look and sighed, left with little choice. "You girls wait here. I'll bring her out." She disappeared through an unmarked door at the opposite end of the rotunda.

Kate wandered off to examine a seascape hanging on the wall. I headed toward a cart near the staircase. It was full of books.

Curious, I read the spines. They were works by German authors. Many were printed in their original language. Goethe.

Gryphius. Jacobi. Klopstock. Kafka. Stramm. Schiller. I tugged at a volume.

The Writings of Kant. We'd been reading Kant that day when Miss Abernathy had told us school was closed. *Enlightenment . . . demands nothing more than freedom—the freedom that consists in making public use, under all circumstances, of one's reason,* I remembered, and I couldn't believe I'd been in a classroom less than a week ago. So much had happened since then. I wondered how Grace was doing in Florence. And how much trouble Margaret was in with her parents. I hoped Fanny was safe. I hoped Emily wasn't too lonely and that Greta's eyes were staying put. I didn't know if anyone else would take the time to sew them back on. I told myself I would write to Grace. Tonight. Or tomorrow. As soon as I had a moment to spare.

A man materialized beside me. He was in his twenties but already balding, with a belly that strained against the fabric of his red sweater. He gave me a sour look, plucking the book from my hands and returning it to the cart. "Excuse me." His voice was strangely high-pitched. "These books are *not* for public use."

"Why not?" I asked, taken aback by his unfriendly tone.

"Because they're *German,*" he said, the same way one would have said, "Because it's *poison.*"

"You're taking away all the German books?" I glanced at the cart. "Even the music books? For how long?" *Until the war ended?* I wanted to know. *Or forever?*

His answer was to sneeze. Directly in my face. The sound echoed throughout the rotunda, and the spray misted around me even as I tried to avoid it. I'd forgotten my mask. I wiped my cheek with my coat sleeve and gave him the dirtiest look I could manage.

Kate appeared by my elbow. "You need to be more careful!" she scolded, pointing a finger at him. Her voice rang out loud and indignant.

The throat clearing coming from the reading room was loud and indignant too. I glanced over. Behind the circulation desk, Miss Tarbell glared at us.

"Sorry," the man said, without sounding sorry at all. He pushed the cart toward the reading room. Short, wheezing pants followed in his wake.

Kate scowled after him before offering me a handkerchief. "Some people should be rationed more than others," she said in a low voice.

"Ugh." I took the handkerchief, scrubbing my face as best I could. The stranger's breath had been rank, his spit equally so, and I wondered how long it would be before I could stick my face beneath a faucet.

The door opened. Mrs. MacMillan appeared with the new children's librarian, whom I'd never met. She was young. Most of her straight black hair had escaped from its roll, straggling around her face. Mrs. MacMillan looked like she was going to topple right over trying to keep her upright. Kate and I rushed to help. I draped one of the librarian's arms over my shoulder. Kate did the same with the other.

The children's librarian looked at Kate, her expression dazed. "Thank you," she whispered.

"You're very welcome," Kate said.

She turned to me. "Thank you," she said.

"Of course. It's nothing," I said.

The children's librarian looked at the floor. "Thank you," she said.

Kate and I exchanged a look. Excited whispers drifted over from the reading-room crowd, though no one approached. Mrs. MacMillan, teary-eyed, told us to be careful. We dragged the librarian down the staircase, past the marble columns, and out of the hush.

The *Evangeline* was to arrive at the dock at two o'clock sharp. As it always did. Today it would be carrying Mrs. Foster, and I planned to drive down to the river and surprise her. I knew she was expecting to find her own way home. As far as she was concerned, I was still at St. Helen's.

I dropped Kate off at the Auditorium and promised Hannah I would be back the next morning. I would, no matter how much Mrs. Foster railed and threatened. I knew I was in for it, that I would receive a terrible tongue-lashing once she learned what I'd been up to. But right now, I was too happy to care.

Good food. Clean clothes. A familiar face. Knowing there was someone else in the house while I slept. Simple things that I would never take for granted again.

I drove home for a quick lunch. Parking out front, I cast a wary glance at the sky. It looked like rain. Which reminded me, I needed a new umbrella. My old one lay crumpled and broken on the rear seat, having lost the battle against Sunday's rainstorm.

"Hello!" a voice behind me called.

I turned. A blond boy, no more than thirteen, rolled toward me on a bicycle. He wore a blue courier's uniform with gold buttons. He slowed to a stop.

"Hello," I said. "A telegram?"

"Two, miss." The boy pulled identical yellow envelopes from a battered leather satchel. He glanced at both. "Are you Luciane or Cleo Berry?"

I eyed the envelopes. Why would someone send Lucy a telegram here? Everyone who knew her was aware of her trip. Knew she wouldn't be home for weeks. "I'm Cleo Berry. I'll take both, thank you."

He handed me the envelopes. "Good day, miss."

The courier pedaled down the street. I opened the telegram addressed to me first. It was from Jack. It read:

CLEO, TELEPHONES ARE USELESS. SEND WIRE—
TODAY—CONFIRMING MRS. FOSTER'S ARRIVAL. NEED
TO KNOW YOU'RE BOTH IN GOOD HEALTH. HOPE TO BE
HOME NEXT WEEK. LUCY IS WELL AND SENDS HER LOVE.
I'M SENDING MINE TOO. JACK.

I smiled. Opening the second telegram, I saw that it had originated in Hood River, from someone named Hazel Balogh. I'd
never heard the name before. I read:

DEAR MRS. LUCIANE BERRY, ADELINE FOSTER TAKEN TO
HOSPITAL WITH ENTIRE FAMILY. INFLUENZA. CONDITION
SERIOUS. I AM THE FOSTERS' NEIGHBOR. CORRESPOND
AT ABOVE ADDRESS. SINCERELY, HAZEL BALOGH.

My hand trembled as I reread the telegram. *Oh no oh no oh no
oh no.* Mrs. Foster. The entire family? I pictured the photographs
cluttering her sitting room. Her grandchildren were very young. A
boy and a girl. Toddlers. *Condition serious.*

I read the note a third time. Then I looked at my brother's telegram. I needed to reply today. If I didn't, he and Lucy would assume
the worst. They would come home. Lucy would insist on it, despite
her condition and in one of the crowded trains with their stagnant
compartments. It was dangerous. But if I told Jack about Mrs. Foster, if he learned I was alone, they would come back anyway.

Leaning against the car, I stared across the street at the Pikes' house. What was I supposed to do? I thought of Mrs. Foster, strict and kind at the same time, who had patched up Jack's skinned knees and mine. And Grace's and Margaret's and Fanny's too. The tears threatened. I blinked them back. *Stop it,* I told myself fiercely. *Stop panicking.* Sick did not mean dead.

I focused, startled when I saw Mrs. Pike standing in her open doorway watching me. She wore a green dress and a white mask. Our neighbor was in her forties. A striking lady, with fair hair and blue eyes. When I was younger, she'd reminded me of the porcelain dolls lining the shelves of the toy emporium. The ones with the blank expressions. The ones that made me grateful for my own scruffy, well-loved doll.

Sniffling, I gave her a small wave. She was the last person I felt like talking to, but I couldn't ignore her. I started across the street, intending to be polite and ask after her health.

Mrs. Pike held up a hand. "Don't come any closer, Cleo," she called out.

I stopped in the middle of the road, surprised. "I won't, Mrs. Pike. Are you well? And Mr. Pike?"

She ignored the question, her eyes fixed on my Red Cross band. "Have you completely lost your senses?" she demanded. "Where is your brother? How could he allow this?"

I stiffened at her tone. In all the years I'd known her, any good-will toward Mrs. Pike had never lasted more than a minute. "Jack and Lucy have been delayed in San Francisco," I said. "I've been volunteering at the hospital."

Mrs. Pike pursed her lips at the news. "I've not seen your housekeeper."

I glanced over my shoulder. Of course she would notice me coming and going at odd hours, and see how few lights were left on in the evening. Turning back, I held up both telegrams. "Mrs. Foster is sick."

Mrs. Pike stared at me for such a time that I was reminded, once again, of those dolls on the shelves. "Then I am sorry for you." My neighbor backed away, into her house, and shut the door.

I'd like to send two telegrams, please. One to Hood River, the other to San Francisco."

"That's fine, miss. Fill these forms out. Be sure to sign at the bottom." The Western Union clerk, an older man with a mask, was polite but brisk.

"Thank you." Using one of the pencils scattered across the counter, I scribbled away, grateful to be at the front of the queue after waiting for two hours. Most of it outside in the rain. At least I hadn't forgotten a new umbrella. Many had, and they'd looked wretched trying to shield themselves with newspapers and brief-cases and purses.

Behind me, the line snaked out the open door. The office was cramped and overheated, and the sounds of traffic drifted in from the street. No one complained. The mood was quiet and sober, with everyone looking downward, preoccupied with their own troubles.

Just like me.

The first telegram was to the kind Mrs. Balogh in Hood River. Explaining who I was. Thanking her for her note. Asking to be kept informed and offering any assistance she could think of. Though, as I wrote the last part, I wondered what I could really do. Even if I took the steamer to Hood River and searched out the Fosters in the hospital, what would I do? Spoon soup? Change sheets? Feeling helpless, I eased my grip on the pencil so I would not snap it in half.

I set Mrs. Balogh's form aside. Behind the counter, more clerks hunched over their desks, typing madly. Through the front window, I could see the Skidmore Fountain. A man stood by the fountain's stone steps, waiting patiently while his horse drank its fill.

The second note was harder. I wrote it quickly, before I changed my mind. And as I signed my name at the bottom of the form, it occurred to me that I didn't used to be such a liar. It wasn't a good feeling, knowing how much I kept from my family. The clerk looked up at my sigh.

"All done, miss?"

"Yes." I handed both forms over, along with my payment,

and watched as they were passed on to one of the transmitting clerks. I accepted my receipt and left, feeling several levels below wretched.

To Jackson Berry, The Fairmont,

San Francisco, California.

Dear Jack, Mrs. Foster is home. We are both well.

Come home when it's safe. Love, Cleo.

CHAPTER SEVENTEEN

Wednesday, October 16, 1918

From the *Oregonian:*

> Deaths yesterday wiped out all but one of a family of four received at the emergency hospital Tuesday—all in delirious condition. Mrs. Godfrey Marshall, who succumbed yesterday, was preceded in death by Carl Marshall, eighteen months of age, and Nina Marshall, eight years, whose fever was one hundred and four when brought to the hospital. Mr. Marshall was removed to the county hospital yesterday. His condition is believed critical. They resided at 123½ Third Street.
>
> A home for two girls of three and six who are convalescent from influenza is being asked by Miss

Waverley Bennett of the American Red Cross. The mother and father still are confined at St. Vincent's Hospital and the children have no place to go.

How the influenza attacks whole families again was illustrated by a report yesterday of eight cases in the family of G. F. Linton, 555 Flanders Street. No deaths yet have been recorded.

Two hundred and seventeen new cases of Spanish influenza were reported to the City Health Bureau, bringing the total number of cases to 1,517. Total influenza deaths number 86.

You think you're smarter than me." I kept my voice low and threatening. "And maybe that's true. But if I wanted, I could take you apart. Piece by piece. I could use you for firewood. What do you say about that, huh? What do you say?"

The washing machine said nothing. It stood there, a useless wooden tub, with its hoses and belts, its cranks and levers. As foreign to me as a submarine. How did Mrs. Foster manage this thing? How did anyone?

I was downstairs at home, in the room used for washing and ironing. A pile of laundry filled the basket by my feet. It was early, not yet five in the morning, but since I couldn't sleep, I thought I might as well attempt the wash. I'd hoped to have some of my clothing cleaned—the bloodiest shirtwaists, the foulest coat—before I left for the hospital. The trouble was I'd never laundered anything before.

I spent some time searching for an instruction manual. Rummaging about the worktable, I found an iron and a small wicker basket filled with needles and thread. Another basket held buttons and ribbons. Above the table, boxes of washing powder and stocking shampoo lined the shelves. Several shirts, draped across the back of a chair, needed mending. But no manual.

Vexed, I studied the washer. The attached wringer looked ominous. I was afraid to go anywhere near it. Wasn't there a girl once who'd caught her fingers in a washer wringer and had them torn right off? Two fingers. It was in all the newspapers. Maybe if I unplugged the washer cord from the socket and plugged it in again? I tried, gasping when a nasty jolt raced up my arm.

"Stupid thing!" I cried, dropping the cord. Grabbing my blue coat from the basket, I flung it at the washer. It hit the tub, before slithering to the floor in a puddle of smelly wool.

I gave up. Thoroughly defeated, I rubbed my arm and slunk upstairs to pour myself a bowl of cereal.

Are you sure you won't change your mind?" Kate asked. "We have plenty of room."

"I can't. I need to spend some time at home," I said, smiling to soften my words. Ever since she'd learned what happened to Mrs. Foster, Kate had been trying to get me to stay with her family. I kept one hand loosely gripped on the steering wheel. "Jack might get through on the telephone. Or a courier might come by. I'd hate to miss them."

"But—"

"Leave her be, Kate," her sister Waverley said from the sidewalk. "She's made up her mind." The head nurse at St. Vincent's Hospital, Waverley was a shorter, plumper, and more serious version of her younger sister.

Kate sighed and gathered her bag and umbrella, joining her sister on the curb. "I'll see you in the morning. Don't be late, or I'll worry."

I smiled. "I won't."

Waverley held the passenger door open. "You'll give Hannah my regards? Tell her I can spare a nurse or two if she still needs them."

"I'll tell her."

"And, Cleo?" Waverley glanced up at the late-afternoon sky, a washed-out gray that was slowly darkening to lead. "It looks like rain, but try to keep these windows open as much as possible."

I promised I would, and Waverley swung the door shut. The sisters disappeared into the hospital.

St. Vincent's was a dramatic-looking building, rising five stories off the ground, with arched windows and dormers lining the rooftop. Unlike the other city hospitals, it was isolated, located high up in the hills and surrounded by rolling fields and farmland.

My mother had spent some time at St. Vincent's, nearly eighteen years ago. I was born there.

Rather than driving off, I leaned back and closed my eyes. Now that Kate was gone, there was nothing to distract me from my own thoughts and worries. I tried to rub the tiredness from my face. A crinkling sound emerged from my coat pocket. I tugged free the copy of *Family Limitation* that Kate had given me yesterday, written by the nurse in New York. Margaret Sanger. I'd forgotten it was there. I opened the leaflet and glanced at a random passage:

IT SEEMS INARTISTIC AND SORDID TO INSERT A PESSARY OR A SUPPOSITORY IN ANTICIPATION OF THE SEXUAL ACT. BUT IT IS FAR MORE SORDID TO FIND YOURSELF SEVERAL YEARS LATER BURDENED DOWN WITH HALF A DOZEN UNWANTED CHILDREN, HELPLESS, STARVED, SHODDILY CLOTHED, DRAGGING AT YOUR SKIRT, YOURSELF A DRAGGED OUT SHADOW OF THE WOMAN YOU ONCE WERE.

I straightened. Quickly, I flipped through the leaflet and read from the very beginning.

WOMEN OF THE WORKING CLASS, ESPECIALLY WAGE WORKERS, SHOULD NOT HAVE MORE THAN TWO CHILDREN AT MOST. THE AVERAGE WORKING MAN CAN SUPPORT NO MORE

AND THE AVERAGE WORKING WOMAN CAN TAKE CARE OF NO

MORE IN DECENT FASHION. IT HAS BEEN MY EXPERIENCE THAT

MORE CHILDREN ARE NOT REALLY WANTED, BUT THAT THE

WOMEN ARE COMPELLED TO HAVE THEM EITHER FROM LACK

OF FORESIGHT OR THROUGH IGNORANCE OF THE HYGIENE OF

PREVENTING CONCEPTION . . .

On and on Mrs. Sanger went, discussing condoms, sponges, douches, and pessaries. There were instructions. There was a picture of a woman's womb. There was a periodical, the *Birth Control Review,* available through subscription for one dollar a year. Sixteen pages in all. Every one of them riveting. Of course I'd heard of condoms before, but only in a vague sort of way, accompanied by giggles and whispers among my schoolmates and Margaret in particular. There was nothing unclear about *Family Limitation.* Mrs. Sanger was so explicit that I felt myself turning red, even though there was no one else in the car.

A door slammed. Startled, I shoved the leaflet into my coat pocket. I felt a seam rip. A car was parked in front of me, a familiar figure standing beside it. It was Mr. Lafayette, looking just as dignified and somber as he had that evening outside the Auditorium. Well, I amended with a bemused smile, looking just as dignified as a grown man could while clutching two rag dolls. I followed his gaze.

Edmund came down the hospital steps, a dark topcoat flapping about his knees and a cap pulled low over his head. A little girl was perched in his arms. She could not have been more than three. Just behind them, a girl of about six clutched the hand of an older woman. Both children wore red coats and hats. As the small group approached, I saw that the children were very thin, with straight brown hair and a marked family resemblance.

Edmund spotted me over the toddler's head. A surprised smile lit his features. He said something to the woman. After a curious look in my direction, she took the toddler from Edmund and continued with both children toward Mr. Lafayette. Edmund headed my way.

"Cleo." Edmund leaned in through the open passenger window. "Hello."

"Hello." I looked at the faint smudges beneath his green eyes, at the hair allowed to grow too long, and felt suddenly, inexplicably, out of sorts. I pressed one hand to my stomach to contain the butterflies, dropping it when Edmund glanced down. I gestured toward the girls, who clutched brand-new dolls. "Are those the children from the newspaper?"

Edmund nodded. "I'm never home. Annabelle and Stella will stay there with Mrs. Graham until their parents are well."

"Has no one else offered to take them in?" I asked, unsurprised when he frowned and shook his head no.

"Mrs. Graham is my old nurse," he added, watching as Mr. Lafayette helped the girls into the car. "She likes to think she still is."

We smiled at each other.

"Are you heading back to the Auditorium?" he asked.

I wasn't. I was on my way home, where I planned to take the hottest bath imaginable and then spend the rest of the evening within arm's reach of the telephone. Just in case it actually rang. The Auditorium was clear out of my way.

I nodded. "Would you like a ride?"

"I'd appreciate it. I'll be right back."

Edmund went over and said a few words to Mr. Lafayette, then stuck his head into the rear window before stepping back onto the sidewalk. He waved as the car pulled away. After turning the hand crank at the front of my car, Edmund climbed in. I started the engine.

"Thanks, Cleo. I came with some others, but they've already left."

"Sure." I headed back toward town, turning off Westover Road and leaving the hospital behind us.

Edmund picked something up off the car floor. One of my influenza flyers, it looked like. "You dropped this." He held up the flyer to catch what was left of the afternoon light. "'*Family Limitation* by Margaret Sanger.' Sanger. Isn't she the nurse—?"

Mortified, I snatched the leaflet out of his hand and flung it over my shoulder, toward the rear seat. Only the windows were all open. The birth control guide flapped in the wind, like a startled chicken, before being whipped right out of the car.

Edmund turned and watched the leaflet fly away. I could not look at him. Both hands gripped the steering wheel. The stupid leaflet had fallen from my stupid coat. What must he think of me? That I was fast? But I wasn't! "It was Kate's." I blurted out the only thing that came to mind.

"Was it?" I could tell he was trying not to smile. "I think it would be fine, even if it wasn't Kate's." He looked over his shoulder again. "I've read all of her books. Hannah has them in her office."

"The ticket office?" I asked, baffled.

Edmund laughed. "No, on Marquam Hill. Hannah runs the nursing program there. It's right next to the medical school. It's how I met her."

I slowed the car, waiting as two brown cows ambled across the road. "Will she get in trouble?" I asked, worry for Hannah over-shadowing my embarrassment. I knew a little about the Comstock laws, which made it illegal to distribute obscene material. Didn't that include information on contraception?

Edmund shrugged. "She doesn't hand out anything. She just leaves her door open and lets everyone know they can make themselves comfortable." Mercifully, he changed the subject. "Any word on your Mrs. Foster?"

I shook my head. I'd surprised Edmund and Hannah when I had returned to the hospital the night before, instead of spending the evening with Mrs. Foster as I'd planned. I'd changed bedding and fed patients and scrubbed dishes until Hannah had ordered me home around midnight.

"Cleo, I was thinking . . . My aunt Clarissa lives with my father. Over on Davis. You could stay with them until your family comes home. They'd be happy to have you."

I glanced at him. "You've already asked them?"

Edmund wouldn't look me in the eye. "There's plenty of room. And they know you're helping out at the hospital. You could come and go whenever you liked."

Kate had offered up her own family home. And now Edmund had as well. It dawned on me that had it not been for the influenza, I would not have met either of them.

"I drive around all day, and everything looks different," I said, trying to explain. "The Auditorium looks nothing like it used to. There are circus tents outside County. And everywhere I go, people are wearing masks. But at home . . . nothing's changed. It's the only place I recognize."

Edmund's silence was followed by a long, frustrated sigh. "Will you let me know if you need anything, at least? Firewood? You won't try and chop down a tree all by yourself?"

His words, and his disgruntled expression, made me smile. "I promise. I wouldn't know where to start."

I drove on. Houses appeared, growing closer together as we reached town. I passed six automobiles, far fewer than normal, even for this time of day.

Edmund peered out the window, then straightened. "Cleo, stop, will you? Right here." He pointed to the side of the road.

Frowning, I did as he asked. "Why?" I looked around.

We were outside the cemetery. I could see headstones through the iron railing, outlined in the dusk and protected by great weeping willows. And then I saw what had caught Edmund's attention. A lantern had been set on the grass, just inside the gates, illuminating a small patch of earth. A man thrust his shovel into the ground, tossing the dirt clumps behind him. He stopped to glance over at us, then resumed digging.

"Do you know him?" I asked.

"No, but I don't think he's a gravedigger. At least not a regular one."

I leaned forward to get a better look. The man was dressed not in the old work clothing you would expect a person digging dirt to wear, but in trousers and shirtsleeves and a vest.

I scanned the cemetery. Eighty-six people had died so far. As much as I tried not to think about it, I knew there would be more. There should have been men here, preparing the graves. There wasn't another soul to be found.

"I don't understand," I said. "Where are the gravediggers?"

Edmund removed his cap and set it on the seat. "Most of them are sick. We have two at the Auditorium. And the others won't go near the bodies."

His meaning sank in. "Are people burying their own family?" I asked. "But that's hideous!"

Edmund nodded. "They don't really have a choice. There's a waiting list for burials, and it's getting longer and longer." With that bit of horrifying news, he opened his door and climbed out. After a second's hesitation, I followed. We walked through the cemetery's ornate arched entrance.

The man had stopped shoveling to watch our approach. He was in his thirties, older than Jack, and slight. His dark hair and mustache were neatly trimmed, but his face was already streaked with dirt and mud. I didn't know how long he'd been here. I hoped not long, because he'd barely managed to unearth a foot of dirt. I looked from the sad little pit to the stranger, wondering whose grave it was meant to be. A parent? A wife? *Please,* I thought, *not a child.*

Edmund and I stopped just shy of the unfinished grave. "Sir. My name is Edmund Parrish. This is Cleo Berry." His tone, suddenly formal, made me think of Sergeant LaBouef.

The man's answering nod was stiff, like a puppet on a string, and his voice was uneven. "Tom Nesbitt," he said.

Edmund gestured toward the extra shovel that lay beneath a

nearby tree, alongside the lantern and a silver flask. "I'd be glad to help."

The light was fading fast, but still I saw the tears that sprang to Mr. Nesbitt's eyes at Edmund's offer and his valiant effort to blink them away. I was as startled as Mr. Nesbitt. I looked around the graveyard. The wind had picked up, gathering the leaves and sending them rustling over the stone markers. I moved closer to Edmund and felt his hand rest against the small of my back.

"I'd be obliged," Mr. Nesbitt said. "My brother would have been here, but . . . he's feeling poorly." He looked down at the grave. "It's for my wife."

My own eyes welled up in response. "I am very sorry, Mr. Nesbitt," I said.

He acknowledged my words with another nod. "They told me she couldn't be buried for two weeks. That's how long I'd have to wait while my Elizabeth . . ." He stopped. "So I said I'd do it myself." He walked slowly over to the tree, reaching for the shovel.

"Oh, Edmund," I said softly.

"Yes" was his quiet response. He looked into my upturned face. "Will you tell Hannah where I am?"

I stared at him. "No. I'm staying here. I'll wait for you," I said.

But Edmund was already shaking his head. His hand dropped from my back. "You're not." He was adamant. "This is going to take hours."

The lantern's glow sent long, twisting shadows across the grass.

"Edmund, it's nearly dark. This is a graveyard." I kept my voice low, not wanting Mr. Nesbitt to hear. Thankfully, he was taking his time, allowing us some privacy.

Edmund's smile was grim. "I'm not afraid of these ghosts, Cleo. I have enough of my own to keep me company."

I wanted to ask him what he meant. Standing there, with the wind blowing hair into my eyes, I wanted to know everything about him. About his family, his friends. About his dream of becoming a doctor. About the war in France. I wondered why there was always something sad around his eyes even when he smiled. I wanted to ask about all these things, but Mr. Nesbitt was making his way back with the shovel. Now was not the time. And so I asked, instead, "What if it rains?"

Edmund was already shucking off his coat. "Then I'll stop." His voice softened. "I won't do anything foolish. You know I can't leave him here."

"I know." There was nothing else to do but agree. Edmund tossed his coat to the ground and took the shovel. After bidding farewell to Mr. Nesbitt, I walked out of the graveyard, into the night, leaving Edmund to dig a grave for a perfect stranger.

CHAPTER EIGHTEEN

Wednesday, October 16, 1918

For the next few hours, I fed any patient who showed the slightest interest in eating. Up and down the stairs I went, with bowl after bowl of watery chicken soup. Hannah asked if I would help her in the ticket office. I did that too. We sat at the desk across from each other, folding a mountain of linen that had just been sent over from the laundry.

The entire time I watched the clock. The hour struck eight, then nine. With each passing minute, I grew more anxious and fidgety, until Hannah finally said with some exasperation, "Stop worrying, Cleo. He'll be here."

"I wasn't worrying."

Hannah raised an eyebrow. "No?" But even she glanced at the clock with a frown. "We'll give him another half-hour, and then I'll send Sergeant LaBouef to fetch him."

I looked at her, grateful. "You will?"

"Yes. Now fold."

I told myself I could put Edmund out of my mind for thirty minutes. We continued folding the bedding and towels, which ranged in color from bright white to worn gray. After a few minutes of companionable silence, I said, "Hannah?"

"Hmm?"

"Do you like being a nurse?"

Hannah looked surprised. "I would wish for a little less excitement than we've had. But, yes, I like it most days. Why? Are you thinking of becoming a nurse?"

"Oh, I . . . no. I don't think I'd be very good at it."

Hannah lowered a towel, frowning. "Why do you say that?"

I shrugged, wishing now that I had kept silent. "I've seen the things that you and the other nurses have to do—"

"What things?"

"Well . . ." I looked toward the ticket window, though the waiting room was closed for the night. "You've had to tell people that someone they love is dead, or dying. You're always calm, even when they start to cry. Even when they start screaming at you. I would fall to pieces if I had to do that."

"I didn't start off knowing how to talk to patients or their families. It takes practice. I've fallen to pieces many times, I promise you."

I gave her a skeptical look, then said, "And everywhere you

turn, someone is bleeding or vomiting or having a needle poked in their ear . . . It's awful. I don't think I have a strong enough stomach to work in a hospital."

Hannah smiled. "Don't you?"

"No, and—" I broke off, struck by a sudden, unpleasant thought. Edmund knew he wanted to be a doctor. He'd always known it. It was the same with Kate and her piano. And Jack had always intended to follow the same path that our father and grandfather had taken. Then there was me. And the unsettling realization that perhaps I was not meant to *be* anything at all. "I'm not like you, Hannah. I'm just . . . ordinary."

Hannah's eyes were fixed on me. "Cleo, how many of your schoolmates do you see here? Wearing that armband?" She shook her head at my blank look and would have said more, I was sure, but one of the soldiers stuck his head in the door.

"Ma'am?" It was the freckled soldier, the skinny one. He looked agitated.

Hannah was already on her feet. "What's wrong, Andrew? Where's your sergeant?"

He acknowledged me with a quick nod. "He's out back. He wanted me to ask if you'd come? As soon as you could?"

Hannah was nearly out the door when she threw a "Come with me, Cleo" over her shoulder. I dropped the towel onto the desk and rushed to catch up.

"What happened?" Hannah demanded as we bypassed the men's ward and hurried directly backstage.

"Freddy—I mean Private Nolan—and I were out back unloading supplies. He tripped coming down from the truck. Landed pretty hard," Andrew said.

"On his head?" Hannah asked.

"No, ma'am. His arm. It doesn't look right."

Hannah looked relieved. I couldn't blame her. An injured arm didn't sound so bad. Not after everything I'd already conjured up in my imagination. We held our silence as we walked by the dressing rooms, knowing some were resting up before they started late shifts.

We pushed through a set of doors and found ourselves in a narrow alley. A truck was parked at the bottom of the staircase. The lighting wasn't as bright as in the front of the building, but it was still enough to see the man sitting at the very back, legs hanging off the sides. Sergeant LaBouef was with him. A trio of soldiers hovered a few feet away, looking queasy. As I followed Hannah around the sergeant's massive form, I saw why.

Despite the bitter night air, Private Freddy Nolan's shirt uniform had been removed. He was stripped down to a sleeveless white undershirt. I winced when I spotted the large bump protruding from his shoulder, beside his collarbone. I had to agree with Andrew. This arm did not look right. I backed away to stand with the other soldiers.

Sergeant LaBouef looked more annoyed than worried. "Fool was monkeying around and fell out of the truck," he said to Hannah. "Looks like it's dislocated."

"It certainly does." Hannah studied the arm. "How are you feeling, Freddy?"

He unclenched his jaw long enough to say, "Like hell, ma'am."

Sergeant LaBouef gave him a look but must have felt some pity in his heart, because he held his peace.

"I imagine you do. Andrew?" Hannah said.

He stepped forward. "Yes, ma'am?"

"There's a sling in my office. To the right of the door, bottom shelf. Please bring it here."

"Yes, ma'am." He trotted up the steps and into the building.

Hannah glanced over her shoulder and beckoned someone forward. I turned to the three soldiers, to see which one she was calling. They were all looking at me. Uncertain, I turned to Hannah.

"Me?" I asked.

"Cleo" was Hannah's impatient response. She moved aside so that I could stand directly in front of Private Nolan. Sympathy stirred within me. I was close enough now to see the sweat beading on his forehead and the pain clouding his eyes. The bump at his shoulder looked red and angry. I would have liked to pat his good arm, to offer some comfort, but I was afraid to touch him. Sergeant LaBouef looked on quietly.

"Hey, Freddy," I whispered.

"Hey," he said, grimacing.

Hannah clasped both hands behind her back. "Private Nolan's shoulder needs to be put back in its rightful place." Her calm, measured tone made me think of Miss Abernathy during our morning lectures.

"Yes?" I wondered what any of this had to do with me.

"His arm is unbent, as it should be," Hannah continued as though I hadn't spoken. "The first step is to take hold of his elbow." She looked at me expectantly.

Horrified, I stepped back, understanding too late her intentions. "You . . . you're not serious!"

"I am perfectly serious. Stop dawdling. He's hurting."

She was right. Freddy's head had dropped forward. He sat there, breathing heavily through his nose, like a bull. I looked behind me. The soldiers blocked the alley. Running would be fruitless. I sent a last desperate glance toward Sergeant LaBouef, but he only lifted his shoulders, his expression clearly asking, *What can I do?*

Enough. I was wasting time. I reached for Freddy's elbow, snatching my hand away when he gasped.

"No, it's all right," he said, sounding shaky. "I'm fine. I'm fine."

I gripped it again, gently, and looked at Hannah. I'm certain I must have looked as terrified as I felt, but she didn't appear to notice. She said, "I want you to bend his arm at the elbow, slowly. His upper arm must be kept perfectly still."

I did as she instructed, listening to his ragged breathing, feeling my own sweat trickle down my neck. "Like this?"

"Yes. Now, rotate his lower arm inward, toward his chest. Slowly. Good. Now outward. There will be resistance, Cleo. It will not feel natural but do not stop. Do it slowly."

My heart thundered in my chest as I pushed Freddy's arm in a direction it was not meant to go. He moaned. Time crawled. I forced the arm outward, outward, until, mercifully, I heard the dull, unmistakable *pop* of a bone settling back into place.

"*Gah!*" Freddy and I cried at the same time. I dropped his arm and stumbled back.

A cheer erupted behind me. Even Sergeant LaBouef cracked a smile. "That will do," I heard Hannah say. "Oh, good, Edmund, you're back. Andrew, the sling, please."

I spun around. Edmund stood there, dirt streaking his face, his shirtfront soaked with mud and grime, his hair stiff with sweat. "We'll make a doctor out of you yet," he said, smiling. "That was good work."

I smiled back, relief washing over me in waves. Hannah said my name, and I turned, eyes on the ground, not happy with her at all. Feeling as though she'd played a dirty trick on me. Until she lifted my chin and said, so softly that only I could hear, "There. You see? You think you're ordinary, but you're the only one who does."

CHAPTER NINETEEN

Thursday, October 17

TO

Sunday, October 20, 1918

The days tumbled one into the next. Kate and I traveled over every inch of our city. North and south, east and west. A hundred times we crossed the Willamette. I welcomed the exhaustion brought on by nightfall, for there was little energy left over to think.

One evening I stopped by Margaret's house. A masked housemaid I did not recognize told me that the Keseys were not accepting visitors. When I inquired if the family was well, I was told they were "well enough" and asked to please be on my way. I left, thinking of how much had changed in a few short weeks. Margaret and I had been friends since we were five. I had always been welcome in her home. Until today.

There was no word from my brother. There was no news from Hood River.

We heard rumors of a vaccine, of trains heading our way with some sort of miraculous cure. But as far as I could tell, that was all it was. Talk and hearsay. Meanwhile, the patient count ticked steadily upward, an average of two hundred new cases a day.

I stopped reading the newspaper when I began to recognize some of the names printed on the death lists. Meg Bailey, the counter girl at the Royal Bakery, who always remembered I liked my tuna salad on pumpernickel, along with a macaroon and a glass of lemonade. Mr. Pressman, the florist, who was never without a smile on his face and a red carnation in his lapel. Marcus Ohle, my schoolmate Louisa's older brother. The last time I'd seen Marcus was in August, playing tennis, looking so handsome in his duck pants and straw hat.

And then there was Jamison Jones, whom I'd never even had a chance to speak to. He passed on early one morning, two hours after his mother.

When I was seven, I followed a stray kitten across the street and into the shrubbery by the Pikes' back veranda. It was a rare dry, beautiful spring day. The daffodils and tulips were just emerging after a long, wet winter. I could see Mrs. Pike through a gap in the rhododendrons, enjoying tea and cakes with several women.

They did not see me.

At dinner that evening, I asked Lucy what the word *syphilis* meant. Lucy's eyes rounded. Her soupspoon hung suspended in midair. Her mouth gaped in a rare display of gracelessness.

Jack also stopped eating. His expression, however, was calm. "Why do you ask, Cleo?"

I lifted my shoulders. "I heard Mrs. Pike tell her friends that she wouldn't be surprised if Jackson Berry has syphilis on account of his wild university days, and is it any wonder his sad little wife is barren."

I heard Lucy's sharp intake of breath, saw her eyes fill with tears. I stared at her, bewildered. What had I done?

Jack looked thunderous. "I'm going to smother that woman!" Throwing his napkin on the table, he shoved his chair back and stood.

Lucy held up one hand and shook her head. "No, Jackson, please." They exchanged a look before my brother dropped into his chair, scowling. His fists were clenched on either side of his plate.

My eyes darted back and forth between them. "What did I say? I'm sorry, Lucy."

Lucy turned to me, smiling gently. "Come here, darling." She slid her chair back.

I wrapped my arms around her, felt her chin rest on my head.

"You didn't do anything wrong, Cleo," Lucy said. She took a deep breath. "Syphilis is a terrible sickness a man can get when he's had too many sweethearts." Jack snorted. Lucy ignored him and continued. "Jackson does not have syphilis, darling. And barren means a woman is not able to bear a child. What Mrs. Pike said *is* true, though it was unkindly put."

I pictured Mrs. Pike sitting on her porch, teacup in hand, laughing at my family. My hands balled into fists.

From that day on, I followed Lucy's example, treating Mrs. Pike with a polite indifference that was as cold as a winter dip in the Pacific. Jack didn't bother with civility. Each time we crossed paths with Mrs. Pike, my brother blasted her with such a nasty look, I once saw her take a step back.

Still, I took no pleasure in seeing her now, thrashing about on a stretcher. Two men maneuvered her into the waiting ambulance. I glimpsed long, fair hair crusted with filth and a face as pale as the moon before the doors slammed shut.

I ran toward the front of the ambulance. "Mr. Briggs!" I called.

The driver was getting ready to close his own door. He stopped when he heard me.

"That you, Cleo?" A pencil was lodged above each ear. I had seen him just that morning, enjoying a cup of coffee in the Auditorium kitchen.

"Yes, sir." I gripped the door with one hand.

He scratched his beard. "It's getting close to dark. Hannah have you working the hill?"

"No, sir. I live here." I pointed at my house. "Please, what happened?" I could see other neighbors, Judge and Mrs. Whelan, old Mr. Hewitt, watching from their porches. No one approached.

Mr. Briggs glanced toward the Pikes' handsome Victorian. "We got a call from a man named Pike, saying his wife had the influenza. Told us to drive to this address and go straight on in without knocking. So we did. Found the poor lady upstairs in the hall. Looked like she was possessed by the devil."

My hand flew to my throat. "What about Mr. Pike?"

Mr. Briggs shrugged. "Gone. Told the telephone operator he could be reached at the Portland Hotel if there was news."

I was dumbfounded. "He . . . he called for an ambulance, and then *left her here?*"

"Happens all the time." But his sour expression suggested that he did not think much of Sterling Pike. "People scared of their own family." Two loud thumps sounded from the back of the truck. They needed to go. I moved to the curb. Mr. Briggs closed his door and started the truck. "Still, it's a helluva thing," he said, leaning out the window so his words could be heard over the engine. "All that money, and there's not a soul willing to care for you when you need it."

For the first time ever, my school gates were closed to me. I peered through a gap in the wrought iron at St. Helen's Hall, waiting for someone to notice me. Waiting for someone to come out. Because I could not go in.

Ten minutes later, the main doors opened. Miss Elliot crossed the lawn at a fast clip. She wore a black coat and no hat. The wind pulled white tendrils from her bun. An umbrella doubled as a walking stick. It was unsettling to see my headmistress with a mask. She stopped well short of the gate.

She stared at me for a long time, not saying a word. She looked at my armband. At the dusty car parked behind me. She scrutinized my face, and I could tell she did not like what she saw. I felt like a completely different person from the girl who had snuck off from school. I knew I looked different too. Thinner, scruffier. Like someone who slept too little and worried too much. I forced myself not to fidget.

Miss Elliot finally spoke. "Twenty years ago, one of my girls joined the circus. She left school at fifteen and married a lion tamer. And now you, apparently, have joined the Red Cross. During an influenza epidemic. I'm not sure which is more disconcerting."

I released a long, pent-up breath. "I'm sorry for running away, Miss Elliot. I'm sorry for not leaving a note. I didn't mean for you to worry."

Miss Elliot raised both eyebrows. "Well, I'm sure we'll address that specific incident when the dust has settled. But I think we have more pressing concerns. What are you doing here, Cleo? I spoke with your brother. He said you would be staying with family friends."

"There was a change of plans." I told her everything. When I finished, I felt a whole lot better and Miss Elliot looked a whole lot worse.

The wind picked up. I pulled my scarf higher, covering my chin. "I wanted to come by and see how you were. The newspaper didn't have anything useful. Is everyone all right?"

"Our quarantine isn't working as well as I'd hoped."

It was what I'd been afraid of. "How many?" I asked.

"We've had four girls fall ill. They're being kept isolated in the infirmary."

"Which girls?" It shouldn't matter. I knew everyone in the school. But I also knew which students had stayed behind, their families too far away to come for them.

"Josie Brandt, Phoebe Duff, Anne Nord." Miss Elliot hesitated. "And Emily Tobias."

My shoulders sagged. Emily. I thought of a rag doll with button eyes. "Is it very bad?"

Miss Elliot looked, once again, at my armband. "I think you can imagine," she said quietly.

"And Emily?"

"Her temperature is one hundred and three. It's been the same for two days. Miss Jenkins is here, and we've hired three private nurses, all highly qualified. We are doing all that we can, Cleo. And we are praying."

Four nurses for four girls. I thought of Hannah, having to do with so much less. Forcing the thought aside, I said, "Yes, ma'am."

We spoke for a few more minutes. I promised Miss Elliot I would be careful. And then I climbed in my car and drove off, more troubled than when I'd arrived.

Do you ever think of walking away? Just leaving this all behind?" I asked.

"Every day," Edmund said. We were finishing our dinner on the upper balcony. Mr. Lafayette had delivered another basket.

I was surprised by his answer. "Truly?"

Edmund set his napkin on the armrest. "I'd leave through the alley. No one would see me go. I could drive home, pack a bag, my fishing rod, and leave town before Dr. McAbee or Hannah even noticed. Head to the mountains maybe. Or the coast."

"You've planned your escape route?" I asked, nonplussed.

"That's right."

"Then why stay?"

Edmund shrugged. "It would be easy enough to leave. But I wouldn't be able to come home again, would I? Not with my head held up."

I thought about that. *"Conscientia mille testes,"* I said. Conscience is as good as a thousand witnesses.

Edmund's eyebrows rose. "I think that's true. You're studying Latin?"

"A little. It was on a test."

He rested his elbows on his knees, watching the patients below. "I was stabbed five times, Cleo. I keep thinking I never should have made it home from France. At the very least, I shouldn't be able to use this hand." He was silent for a few moments. "I figure every day I've had since then is a windfall."

"A second chance?" I asked softly.

He glanced over and smiled. "Maybe so. I know it's going to get worse before it gets better. The smart thing to do would be to run for the hills. But I look at everyone down there, and do you know what I tell myself?"

I shook my head.

"I tell myself they're alive. I tell myself they're still breathing. And that means there's still hope."

Hello? Mr. Eba? Mrs. Eba?"

I stood just inside the store, the tinkling of the bell fading above me, and knew instantly that I was alone. A stillness hovered in the air, just beneath a layer of onions and gingersnaps and the merest hint of wet dog.

I'd been on my way home when I saw the lights blazing from the Eba Grocery and Provisions Store. A lucky thing; I was out of cereal, which I planned to eat for both dinner and breakfast.

Though Mrs. Foster preferred Butters Grocery near the house, I'd met the Ebas once or twice. They were nice people. And I was lucky to find any store open at this hour. The other businesses on the street—the greengrocer, the fishmonger, the veterinarian clinic—were locked up tight for the night.

But the door had been left ajar. Where was everyone?

I tried again, louder this time. "Hello? Mr. Eba, it's me. Cleo Berry."

Nothing.

The store was stocked with goods ranging from jam jars and coffee cans to candles and matches. To my right were tins filled with spices, tea, and California apricots. A barrel overflowed with peanuts, and, on the floor, open crates displayed green beans, onions, and potatoes. I looked at the counter, where a scale dominated the space beside a telephone. The shelves behind the counter were empty. All of them. Cleared right off. Standing on tiptoe, I looked over the counter, half expecting to see one of the Ebas collapsed on the floorboards. I saw nothing except a few cans of tomato sauce lying on their side.

I hurried toward the back. Above my head, garlic clusters trailed from a wooden pole. I found a tiny office and an even tinier bathroom. Both rooms were empty. Maybe there had been an emergency—no great surprise—and someone had simply forgotten to lock up. It was understandable. I'd done it myself.

I opened the back door and let myself out into the windy

night. Three trash barrels and a delivery truck crowded the alley. Just to be sure, I checked the truck. Empty.

I'd left the back door open. When the bell sounded from the store, I was relieved. The Ebas must have just stepped out. I was growing too panicky, sensing disaster around every corner, working myself up for nothing. I retraced my steps and was almost inside when I heard unfamiliar voices. Two women.

"The spices first. Then the coffee. Quickly, girl!"

"But what if someone happens by, Mrs. Lily?" The second voice was high-pitched. Younger and frightened. "They'll throw us in jail for sure! I don't think it's right, stealing from the sick."

I froze.

"No one will happen by," Mrs. Lily snapped. "The entire family's been shipped off to St. Vincent's. And I'm not paying you wages to think, Delilah. Now, lift your feet!"

I crept toward the door and peeked in.

Two women ransacked the store. One in her twenties, the other middle-aged. Both were dressed in dark coats and hats. The older lady was round as a snowman, with pursed lips and a sour expression. Mrs. Lily, I presumed. As I gaped, she lifted a thick arm and cleared an entire shelf of coffee cans into a waiting wheelbarrow. Delilah was scrawny and had the look of a browbeaten servant about her. She jumped at the sound of the coffee falling into the barrel, nearly dropping an armful of spice tins.

Neither woman noticed me. I stood in the doorway, unable to remember the last time I'd been this angry.

"I said the candles and the matches! Not the spices. Stupid girl!"

Delilah flinched. She put down the spices and gathered some candles.

I'd had enough. "I beg your pardon," I said.

The women whirled. Delilah squeaked, dropping the candles. The white tapers dented as they hit the wood and rolled across the floor in every direction. Mrs. Lily's face turned an unflattering shade of puce. Both pairs of eyes fell on my Red Cross armband.

I'd been taught to respect my elders, to never raise my voice, to never sass, no matter what. Just this once, though, I was sure Lucy would forgive me.

"What are your names?" I asked, trying my best to imitate Hannah, sharp and no-nonsense. I thought of my own names for them.

Looters. Vultures.

Delilah stared at her worn shoes. Mrs. Lily sniffed. I could see she'd disregarded the armband. Had only seen how young I was and judged me no more threatening than the quivering Delilah.

"I'm sure that's not your concern, miss." Mrs. Lily drew herself up. "Come along, Delilah." She lifted the handles of her wheelbarrow, still filled with stolen goods, and pushed it toward the front door.

"Ma'am," I said quietly. "If you take those, I will follow you to your home. And then I will drive directly to the police station."

Mrs. Lily halted, her back toward me. There was a moment of tense silence.

Delilah twisted her hands. "Mrs. Lily?" she whimpered.

"Shut up, girl!" Without looking my way, Mrs. Lily tipped the wheelbarrow. Goods toppled to the floor. It was a mess. "Let's go," she barked, then hustled out the door. Delilah followed.

The bell tinkled.

I stepped over candles and coffee, and peered out the front window. Two shadows hurried down the street. Turning, I planted my hands on my hips and surveyed the room. Infuriated was too mild a word to describe how I felt. I didn't know how sick the Ebas were, or if they would return anytime soon. But one thing was certain. I could not let them come back to this.

Lord, I was hungry. I'd only stopped in for some cereal.

I tossed my coat on the counter. Pulled off my hat. I rolled up my sleeves and got to work.

CHAPTER TWENTY

Monday, October 21, 1918

No fever," Edmund said.

Tess Cooke lay on her cot, her hair spread against a thin, stingy pillow. She looked from her son, lying half asleep on his own bed, to the thermometer in Edmund's hand. Her eyes filled with tears.

"He has no fever?" she asked, her voice more rasp than whisper. "You're sure?"

Edmund smiled. "I'm certain. I checked twice."

I stood beside Tess's bed, a sleeping Abigail in my arms. Tess still had a slight fever, but her nosebleeds had stopped, and she was able to keep down more food than she threw up. Finally, some good news.

Edmund reached for Abigail. "Can you spare her, Cleo?"

I handed Abigail to him and turned to Tess. "I could come

and help with the children, if you like," I offered. "Even after you leave here, you won't be on your feet for some time."

Tess smiled. "You've done so much already. Charlie's on his way. And my sister will come too."

A wire had arrived yesterday. Mr. Cooke had been located laying railroad tracks in some godforsaken desert in Arizona. He would be home tomorrow. I smiled back, relieved for her.

Edmund pulled the stethoscope from his ears. "Abby's temperature is normal. And her lungs are clear. It looks like we just might be over the worst of it."

I peered over his shoulder, anxious. "Her lungs are fine? How can you be sure? It's not as if she can tell you how she's feeling."

Edmund exchanged a glance with Tess. "I can't be. But when a patient has influenza, the lungs make a gurgling sound. And the heartbeat slows dramatically. Put this on. Listen." He pulled the stethoscope from around his neck and handed it to me, still holding Abigail with one arm. I put the stethoscope on, the feel of it strange inside my ears. Edmund pressed the chest piece against Abigail's heart. I listened to the steady beat. He moved the stethoscope over her lungs. I heard nothing. I pulled the stethoscope from my ears. Tess and Edmund looked at me, expectant.

"I think she's over the worst of it," I said.

Tess smiled. I offered Edmund the stethoscope, along with a sheepish glance. Humor glinted in his eyes. He turned toward Tess, and I started down the aisle to give them some privacy.

I smiled at Hannah, who fitted an empty cot with fresh sheets, and wondered when she slept. I passed Dr. McAbee. He peered into a woman's ear with a needle in his hand, and I shuddered in sympathy for her. At the end of the aisle, a nurse named Callie King hung a toe tag on a body.

I averted my eyes. When they passed on, patients were immediately moved downstairs, to the temporary morgue. It was not good for those in the wards to see a body being prepared for burial. But this woman had already been wrapped tight in a white binding sheet. Only her head was left exposed. And one slim foot, for the tag.

I started to walk past. Stopped. My heart stuttered. I approached the bed and wondered if I was seeing things. Callie looked up. I saw now that the body belonged not to a woman, but to a girl, fourteen or fifteen. Without saying a word, I reached down and placed two fingers on the side of her neck. As I did, her eyes blinked open, wide as an owl's.

I fell back with a muffled shriek. The little girl in the neighboring cot shifted but did not wake. Out of the corner of my eye, I saw Edmund's head snap up. I stared across the bed at Callie. Disbelieving. She stood frozen, looking back at me with round, guilty eyes.

"She's still alive," I whispered.

"I'm sorry! I'm so sorry!" Callie said, the circles like smudges of charcoal beneath her eyes. "It's just . . . it saves time. She'll be gone by morning and it . . . it just saves time." She yanked off the tag and pulled at the girl's foot. Trying to undo the binding. She stopped. She began to cry.

Callie looked exhausted. But I was tired too. And outraged. Anger burned within me, a terrible, seething resentment. How dare she give up on her? The girl's eyes had shut, and her lips and face were tinged the color of blueberries. But she was not dead yet.

Hannah appeared, for once looking unsettled. "Come with me, Callie." She put one arm around the nurse and guided her toward the door. Hannah threw a look over her shoulder. "Leave her, Cleo," she said quietly. "I won't be long." They disappeared through the doorway, the sound of Callie's weeping trailing after them.

"Christ." Edmund stood beside me.

I did not look at him. "How do we know she can't hear us?" My voice trembled. "How do we know she didn't feel someone wrapping her up like a mummy? She would have been so scared." I felt around the girl's foot, trying to find the edge of the binding.

Edmund touched my arm. I shook him off.

"Don't," I said. "I won't go. I'm not leaving her like this."

"I'm not asking you to." Edmund walked around me. He gently lifted the girl's head and tugged at the binding behind her neck. Holding up the edge of the cloth, he looked at me, as calm and as steady as ever.

"Here," he said. "Hold her up for me. I'll pull her free."

CHAPTER TWENTY-ONE

Tuesday, October 22, 1918

As it turned out, the rumors were true. There was a vaccine. The lower-level balcony was crowded — with doctors, nurses, soldiers, even Mr. Malette, the cook. We sat in our red leather opera chairs while Dr. Montee explained that a shipment of influenza vaccine had arrived. There was enough to inoculate twenty thousand people.

A murmur filled the space. I exchanged glances with Kate and Edmund, who sat on either side of me. Twenty thousand? That's it? Portland had ten times the number of people. More than ten.

Dr. Montee had been responsible for every flu-related decision made in the past month. Closing the schools. Opening the emergency hospitals. Placing police outside the streetcars to prevent overcrowding. He was a small man with a big job.

The doctor waited until the balcony quieted before he resumed speaking. "I understand your concerns." Though slight, he had a voice that carried. "Twenty thousand is the most we could acquire at this time. I'm hopeful we can obtain more soon. I want to stress that due to the nature of the epidemic, its rapid spread, and the urgency with which this vaccine was devised, the drug has not undergone the rigorous testing that is typical before such widespread dispersal. However, the test results we do have show some success in limiting the influenza's severity. Let me be very clear—it does not prevent Spanish influenza outright, and it is ineffective when used on a patient who has already contracted the flu." Dr. Montee's mask expanded over a frustrated breath. "In other words, my friends, desperate diseases require desperate remedies. This is all we have."

An untested vaccine that was of no use to those already dying. It was not the miracle drug we had hoped for. Far from it.

Hannah stood beside Dr. Montee. I leaned toward Edmund. "Your mask," I whispered.

Edmund glanced quickly at Hannah. She was staring straight at him with narrowed eyes. He pulled his mask over his nose.

Dr. Montee adjusted his bow tie. "Please know that the vaccine is strictly voluntary, though I cannot recommend it enough given your close and continuous proximity to infected persons. There is no charge for those here. The remaining vaccine will be transferred to physicians' offices and to public clinics. The cost is one dollar per vaccine. I suggest you bring your families in immediately." He turned to Hannah. "Mrs. Flynn?"

Hannah stepped forward. "Dr. McAbee will administer the men's shots in the first-floor smoking room," she called. "Ladies, please follow me. You'll receive yours in the exhibit hall on the third floor."

The noise level rose once again as the crowd made its way to the exits. Kate, Edmund, and I were seated in the back row. In the farthest corner. We stayed put, waiting for the crowd to thin.

"I don't like needles," Kate said.

"Neither do I." I turned to Edmund. "Where do they give the vaccine? In the arm? Or . . ." I trailed off, uneasy, thinking of the other place one could get poked with a needle.

Edmund pulled his mask down. He was smiling. "In the arm," he confirmed. "It's a fast shot. You'll hardly feel it."

That was little comfort. "It's barely been tested," I said. "What if it gives us rickets? Or milk leg?"

Edmund's smile widened. "I think we're safe from milk leg." He nudged my shoulder with his. "And better rickets than this flu."

"I guess so." I turned to Kate, who had gone quiet listening to us.

"Kate?" I whispered. I touched her arm.

Kate's palms were pressed against her temple, her eyes glazed over with pain. And her mask. It was no longer white.

It was red.

Swearing, Edmund scrambled to his feet. He yanked at her gauze. Twin rivers of blood flowed from her nostrils, dripping down her chin and onto her blouse and skirt. As Edmund lifted her in his arms, she looked at me.

"My head hurts," she said.

Edmund sprinted toward the women's ward, Kate clutched in his arms. I ran after him. He was pale, Kate even more so. And I remembered Henry Thomas lying on the sidewalk outside the Portland Hotel.

We burst into the room. The nurses—the few left behind while the rest of us received vaccines—barely glanced up. Bleeding patients were common here, and they had their own troubles. In the first aisle, Edmund found an empty cot near the mirrored wall. He set Kate on the bed but wouldn't let her lie down.

"We have to keep her upright for now," he explained tersely. "Or she'll choke."

Kate was crying, her nose still bleeding. I grabbed a clean towel from a cart and did my best to mop her off. "You're going to be fine, Kate," I murmured. "It's only a little blood. You'll be fine." I said it over and over again, trying to keep the panic from my voice.

In the mirror, I caught a glimpse of William Cooke, sitting up for the first time. He held the toy submarine I'd brought him yesterday. A little girl watched us from the next cot. She saw the blood and started to cry. I turned away. Not now, not now.

"Cleo." Edmund's voice was urgent.

"What?" I cried. "What do I do?"

"Get Hannah."

I looked at Kate. Coughing. Her shoulders heaving. I dropped the towel on the bed and ran.

Upstairs in the exhibit hall, a line of women stood with their backs to me. One of the nurses sat in a chair at the front of the queue, her shirtwaist unbuttoned and pushed off one shoulder to expose an arm. Beside her, a frowning Hannah held a long needle up to the light. She tapped the needle with one rigid finger, then smiled with satisfaction when a small stream of liquid emerged. Hannah caught sight of me, and her mouth formed a small O. The other women turned in unison. And I saw the alarm on their faces.

I looked down. At the blood soaking my sweater, my skirt. I reached up and felt the sticky wetness on my cheek.

Hannah was not God. Neither was Edmund. Or Dr. McAbee. Or any of the other medical staff who could do nothing as Kate shivered and cried beneath her blanket. In fact, I thought, rage and fear simmering within me, it was clear God was nowhere near this building.

Around me, the day continued. Edmund was called downstairs to help transport bodies to the morgue. Two soldiers had collapsed right after Kate. We were even more short-handed. Hannah sent Mrs. Howard upstairs to finish the inoculations. She stayed in the ward herself, never too far away. I gathered the extra set of clothes Kate had left in the downstairs comfort station. Hannah and I peeled off her bloody clothing. Threw them in the trash.

"Should we fetch her mother?" I asked. Hannah hated having visitors inside the hospital, allowed them in only to say goodbye. It was not safe. But who was safe? Not the people inside the hospital. Not the people outside. None of us.

Hannah glared at Kate's thermometer. She didn't respond.

"What is it?" I asked.

"One hundred and five."

Our eyes met, and I saw my own anguish reflected in hers.

I gripped Kate's hand beneath the covers, trying to hold back the tears.

"Should we fetch her mother?" I asked again, my voice catching. "Her parents? I can go."

"Not yet."

Kate drifted in and out of sleep. The bleeding had stopped for now, but her hand burned in mine. I thought back to this morning, wondering if I'd missed something. Some sign. But no. She had been fine. I'd brought cinnamon rolls. Kate climbed into the car, smiling as always. Hannah called us back before I'd had a chance to drive off. One of the city health officers was here, Hannah said. He wanted a word with all of us. We didn't eat our breakfast, I realized suddenly. The pastries were still in the car. Was that why? I felt the hysteria bubble up inside of me. Would Kate have fallen ill if she'd had her breakfast?

Hours passed. Hannah was standing beside me. We were looking at Kate. At the dark blue spots on her cheekbones. *Cyanosis,* I thought, remembering my first day at the hospital. Cyanosis. A death sentence.

"Simon," Hannah said quietly.

Sergeant LaBouef was just across the aisle, pulling off soiled sheets. His gaze touched on my still-bloodied clothing before he answered Hannah. "What can I do?" he asked.

"I need you to drive to St. Vincent's. I need you to find Kate's sister. Her name is Waverley Bennett."

The sergeant closed his eyes briefly and nodded. He took the sheets with him as he left.

Hannah touched my shoulder. I covered my face with both hands and wept.

Backstage, in the showers, I bent my head beneath the spray. Not caring that I used a stranger's bar of soap. A sliver of Ivory I'd found on a shelf, with small bits of hair caked in. A

231

week ago, it would have given me the willies. Today I ignored it. I shampooed. I washed. I watched Kate's blood drain away at my feet.

Waverley Bennett was on the way. I didn't doubt Kate's parents were also being notified. And I didn't want her family to see me as I was.

I stayed under the spray for so long the water chilled. When I was done, I dressed in a spare set of clothes I'd left behind after my first experience with the Cookes. The women's shower room was connected to a comfort station, a soft pink room with lit vanities and gold brocade settees. I stopped when I saw Edmund leaning against a wall. We were alone.

I took a deep breath, long and shaky. "Is she . . ."

Edmund straightened. "No. But she's worse, Cleo. Waverley's with her. They've sent for her parents. We can't get through on the telephone." He gestured toward the nearest vanity.

I looked at the tabletop. A single needle rested on a white cloth beside a bottle and some bandaging. My vaccine. Too late for my friend.

I sniffled. Nodded. I sat on a long padded bench in front of the vanity and unbuttoned my shirtwaist halfway down. Enough to pull the cloth off my shoulder. My chemise was exposed, the first time any male other than my doctor had seen my underthings.

Edmund straddled the bench, so close I felt his breath on my skin. He reached for the bottle. It clattered back onto the vanity when I pressed my palm flat against his chest. I needed to feel his heartbeat. To convince myself that he was safe, that he would not fade away right before my eyes. Edmund covered my hand with his. And my name, when he said it, was a sigh. His lips touched mine in a long, slow, sweet kiss. My first. I closed my eyes, feeling his heart beating fast beneath my fingertips.

He lifted his head. "Cleo, wait. I need to do this."

I watched as he fumbled with the needle, the bottle, finally closing his eyes and waiting for his hands to settle. From the next room came the faint intermittent drip of the showers.

"What if it's too late?" I asked.

"Don't."

I felt a pinch, a sharp sting, as the needle entered my arm.

I heard someone crying in the storage closet. The door was ajar. When I looked in, I saw Hannah weeping in Sergeant LaBouef's arms. Rocking and weeping. It was an awful thing to watch and hear. Hannah didn't see me — her face was buried in his shirt — but the sergeant did. He shook his head, once. I nodded, stepped back, and closed the door as quietly as I could.

Kate's skin had taken on the color of lead. Not just her cheekbones. But her entire face, her ears, her neck. She looked like a statue. Except that statues don't shake in their beds so hard that they rattle against the floor.

Digitalis didn't help. Neither did oxygen or codeine. Only morphine helped.

Edmund was called away again. I don't know where. Waverley was by Kate's side, dressed in a Red Cross uniform. Not wanting to intrude, I stayed back, with Tess, holding Abigail in my arms.

Hannah appeared. Her eyes were red, her face splotchy. She placed her hand on my forehead. "Open up," she said, and when I did, she stuck a thermometer beneath my tongue. She glanced at the result and released a pent-up breath. A nurse across the room called for her. Hannah patted my face and was off.

Andrew had gone to fetch Kate's parents. It would take him a while. The Bennetts lived over the bridge, on the eastern edge of town. I watched the door, willing them to walk in.

They did, eventually. They ran in. Mr. and Mrs. Bennett, along with four more sisters. Etta, Ruby, Amelia, and Celeste.

But they were too late.

CHAPTER TWENTY-TWO

Tuesday, October 22, 1918

The rotten car would not start. I tried everything — turning the hand crank, rattling the steering wheel, fiddling with the pedals. Nothing emerged save a series of *pfft-pfft-pfft*s before the automobile fell, once again, into silence.

I opened the door and stepped down. Circling the car — once, twice, three times — I inspected it as if I had the slightest idea of what to look for. Hateful tin can. It would fail me now, when all I wanted in the world was to drive away from this awful place. Drive away and never stop.

I started to climb back into the car. Hesitated. Using both hands, I felt along the edges of the front seat and lifted the upholstery from its frame. For one horrible moment, all I could do was stare at the gasoline tank hidden beneath the seat. Surely not. Surely I could not have forgotten . . . But I *had* forgotten. My telephone conversation with Jack came rushing back to me, along with his reminder to check the gasoline levels. When was the last time I'd been to a filling station?

I reached into the rear seat and retrieved the measuring stick from the floor, then twisted the gasoline cap and set it on the tank. I pushed the stick into the opening, counted to five, and removed it. Just as I feared, the stick came back clean, save a small greasy spot at the tip.

I had run out of gas.

Disgust washed over me. I tossed the stick back onto the rear floor, replaced the cap, and dropped the seat into place. The Auditorium loomed behind me. I would not look at it. I couldn't go back in there, not even to ask for help.

Not today.

Not ever.

I slammed the door shut.

Tugging my coat closed, I walked. Past a group of nurses with pity on their faces. Past the anxious-looking couple hurrying toward the Auditorium steps. Past a soldier pacing on the corner, inhaling his cigarette as if someone were about to snatch it from him.

I walked on.

Hearing nothing.

Seeing nothing.

But Kate.

The rain came before I'd gone a block. A few drops at first, and then a downpour. I didn't turn back. I tipped my face to the sky. Welcomed the coolness on my skin. In this world of mine, it was the rain, it was the rain alone, that made sense.

Night had fallen hours before, leaving the streetlamps to chase the shadows. Shivering, I looked around and realized I had walked clear across town. The Lang & Co. Wholesale Grocery stood dark and shuttered for the night, but beside it the Western Union Telegraph Office still bustled. I could see the men and women queued up through the large front window, a reminder that I'd heard nothing from Hood River. I forced the thought from my mind. Not now. Not now.

In front of the telegraph office, the Skidmore Fountain stood quiet and serene. I sat on the stone edge and swung my shoes inside the fountain. The storm had passed, leaving a small amount of rainwater gathered at the bottom of the basin. I skimmed the shallow water with my toe.

Pushing my dripping hair from my eyes, I studied the statues rising from the fountain's center. Two maidens, their backs aligned, faced opposite directions. Their dresses were gathered in long, draping folds, and their arms were braced high above their heads, holding up a large oval disk. I looked at the one closest to me. The statue's head was slightly lowered. She stared directly at me with impassive eyes. She did not look cold or confused or scared. I envied her lack of emotion. What I would give right now, to feel nothing.

Pale death, the grand physician, cures all pain. I'd thought the saying romantic when I'd first read it in school, but now it just sounded stupid. Whoever had written it had never been inside an influenza hospital. Death cured nothing. Did nothing to ease the pain of those left behind. I thought of Kate's laughter, of her kindness, of her fingers flying across the keys. And I wondered how God could have made such a terrible mistake.

I gasped as a draft whipped through my wet coat. It was a foolish, dangerous thing I had done. I knew it. I needed to go home. And I would have to walk. No conductor would allow me on his streetcar. Not like this. Even if one felt sorry for me, the police officers stationed by the trolleys would override him. I looked toward the west hills. Miles away. Swinging my legs out of the fountain, I tried not to think of the distance.

Headlights flashed through the darkness. I looked away, waiting for the car to pass, but it did not. It came to a sudden, screeching halt in the middle of the street before swinging up onto the sidewalk and stopping within a foot of the fountain steps.

I backed away, nearly tumbling into the horse trough built into the side of the fountain. Catching myself, I threw a hand up to shield my eyes from the lights. The engine was impossibly loud. And scary. I calculated the distance to the telegraph office. The car door swung open, and a tall, dark figure emerged. My shoulders sagged as I realized two things. One, I would not be attacked and left for the dead on the steps of the Skidmore Fountain. And two, I would not have to walk home after all.

Edmund took in my soaked clothing and hair plastered to my head. "You've gone crazy!" he yelled. "Have you gone crazy? I've been driving around for three hours trying to find you!" He stormed toward me, looking madder than I'd ever seen him. He yanked off his coat. Swung it over my shoulders. Squeezed the water from my hair, felt my forehead, my neck. Tipped my head and peered up my nose. Looked in my ears. Blew warm air on my hands. All the while still shouting. "Your car is at the hospital. I thought you were with Hannah. Then I find out you'd walked off into the freezing rain *in the middle of a flu epidemic!* Have you gone crazy?"

I let him holler. I let him finish. And then I asked, tiredly, "Where is she?"

Just like that, the fight drained out of him. He looked away. He shook his head and didn't answer.

"Is she still at the hospital?" I persisted. "Did they take her—?"

"Shhh." He cupped a hand on each side of my face and kissed me. A car sped past, a loud whistle and male laughter trailing behind it. Neither of us looked up.

Edmund rested his forehead against mine before saying, "I took her." His voice was ragged, reminding me I was not the only person today who'd been forced to see and do things they had never dreamed of. "Sergeant LaBouef and I drove Kate to the mortuary. Her father came with us. She was . . . They'll take good care of her."

I stepped back, hand pressed to my mouth, wishing I hadn't asked. "I'm scared I'm going to wake up tomorrow, and you won't be here," I said. "My family. They won't be here. They won't be anywhere."

"I'll be here."

I shook my head, blinking back the tears. "How do you know? You can't."

He reached out and pulled his coat tighter around me. "I will be here," he repeated. "And so will you. And if you care anything about me, Cleo, you will let me take you home. Now."

I nodded. He kept his arm around me, holding me up, and led me to the car.

We were in my kitchen, by the fire, huge mugs of tomato soup in our hands. Canned soup Edmund had heated up while I bathed and put on warm, dry clothing.

"The Cookes will be going home soon," Edmund said.

"Yes."

"And the boy, Mateo Bassi?" he asked.

Surprise flickered through the numbness. I had never mentioned Mateo. Not to Edmund. "He's still at County," I said. "But he doesn't have pneumonia. The doctors think he has a chance."

Edmund nodded as though he already knew. "That first day at the Auditorium, I thought, *I won't see her again. She'll wash her hands of this whole sorry mess, stay home, and bolt the doors. Who can blame her?* But I saw you the next day, and the next, when so many others have walked away."

I looked down at my soup, saying nothing.

He set his mug on a small table. "I know what it's like to lose a friend and wonder why you're the one left behind. To think that nothing makes sense. Not one thing. I know it, Cleo."

Edmund reached out and poked at the fire. I watched the flames dance over his silver watch and his tags, and listened.

"But when you wake up tomorrow and think there's no reason to keep going, to get out of bed and put one foot in front of the other, I hope you remember that William Cooke and Abigail Cooke and Mateo Bassi will grow up simply because you chose to stay the course. It's no small thing."

Outside, the rain came down in torrents.

We sat, warmed by the fire, listening to the distant rumble of thunder.

CHAPTER TWENTY-THREE

Wednesday, October 23, 1918

The sound of an engine woke me. I lifted my head, turning a bleary eye toward my bedroom window. The curtains had not been pulled the night before. The sun had yet to make an appearance. In these moments between dawn and daylight, Mount Hood stood in stark relief against a fading purple sky. I dropped face-first into my pillow.

A car door slammed. There were voices, male voices. I scrambled out of bed, shivering in the morning chill. Goose bumps appeared on my arms. I tugged the quilt free and wrapped it around my shoulders before scurrying across the wooden floor. I peered out the window.

A truck was parked on the curb, the words U.S. ARMY emblazoned across its side. I could see Sergeant LaBouef in the driver's seat, his profile sharp and distinctive. Behind the truck was my own Tin Lizzie, looking as clean and polished as when Jack first drove it home. As I looked on, Edmund stepped from my car dressed in a tan mackintosh and a brown checked cap. He didn't try to smother a yawn. He walked around to the truck's passenger door, then paused, turning to look at the house.

Our eyes met through the glass. I placed one palm against the windowpane before mouthing the words *Thank you.* Unsmiling, Edmund inclined his head. An acknowledgment. The truck roared to life, its engine loud enough to wake the neighborhood. Edmund jumped in. His window remained open. I could see his arm resting on the frame.

Touched, I leaned my forehead against the glass and watched as the truck disappeared down the street.

The courier hurried down my front path, tripping once before climbing on his bicycle. I didn't pay any attention as he pedaled away — I was too focused on the Pikes' home across the street. A sliver of black wool fluttered against their front door. It had been there all morning.

I walked into the house and shut the door.

CLEO, LEAVING TOMORROW. WILL STAY NIGHT IN K. FALLS, BALDWIN HOTEL. HOME FRIDAY. HAVE MRS. FOSTER MEET SO. PACIFIC #13. 7:30. JACK.

Klamath Falls. Jack and Lucy would be in Oregon tomorrow. There was a chair beside the entry table. I sat down, hard, and pressed the telegram to my chest.

The spider was black and hairy, with scuttling little legs that made my skin crawl. I shoved my chair back so fast it nearly tipped over. The spider made its way across the kitchen table and onto my spoon before tumbling into the bowl of oatmeal. Normally, I would have hollered for Jack, who would have coaxed it onto a newspaper and escorted it outdoors. Or screeched for Mrs. Foster, who would have rolled up the same paper and thumped the spider flat. I would not have bothered with Lucy. She would have taken one look and started screaming right alongside me. I eyed the creature floundering in the milk. *This is your lucky day, spider,* I thought. I did not have the heart to watch anything die today.

I folded the front page of the *Oregonian* into a square and set the paper's edge alongside the bowl's rim. Seeing the lifeline, the spider plucked its thin legs from my breakfast and scurried onto a small, grainy photograph of Mayor Baker, who looked as if he were at his wits' end. Tipping the paper downward so the spider wouldn't be tempted to crawl up onto my arm, I opened the back door and knelt, giving the newspaper a gentle shake. The spider jumped onto the porch and scurried between the railings.

It was midmorning. Since waking at dawn, I'd done nothing except think of Kate. And of Edmund. And of Hannah. I wondered how she was making do, with people falling ill all around her. And with volunteers like me, who'd decided they'd had enough and stayed away.

Straightening, I watched my old wooden swing rock in the breeze beneath a gnarled oak tree. Great piles of wet sunset-colored leaves carpeted the ground. Our gardener, Mr. Rose, should have been here by now, raking and preparing the garden for winter. I thought about sifting through Mrs. Foster's telephone numbers and contacting him myself, then dismissed the thought. Even if I could get through, Mrs. Foster would not appreciate my meddling with her routine. She would call Mr. Rose herself when she returned.

Behind me, the kettle whistled. I shut out the cold and tossed the newspaper onto the counter. I set about making my tea. Gathering my cup, I retrieved the newspaper and placed both beside the bowl of ruined oatmeal.

I stared at the paper. Minutes ticked by before I unfolded it and skimmed through until I found the list on page seven. Twenty-nine dead yesterday. More than two hundred in total. A terrible curiosity filled me as I read through the names:

B. B. Armstrong, 39, machinist, 998 East Seventeenth Street.

Zoe Z. Novel, 25, teacher, 853 Upshur Street.
George A. Groshens, 33, fireman, 426 Beech
Street.

It went on. Machinist, teacher, fireman. Lives reduced in print to the barest of facts. Was that really all they had been? There was no mention of their dreams or disappointments, or of the people left behind to mourn their loss. I felt angry at the waste. I started to turn the page when I saw the last name printed on the list.

And I remembered there was another reason I'd begun to shy away from the paper. A part of me had known that, had I continued to look, eventually I would come across a name that would crack my heart wide open. For me, today was that day.

Katherine Bennett, 17, 520 Goodpasture Island
Road.

Kate.
I crumpled the paper with both hands and threw it across the room.

Hannah." I was hovering in the door of the ticket office.
Hannah glanced up from her desk, her eyes widening when

she saw what I held in my arms. "Oh!" She jumped to her feet and crossed the room.

I tightened my hold on the sleeping toddler—a brown-haired, blue-eyed little girl—and spoke in a rush. "I could hear her crying from the porch. No one answered my knock and the doors were all locked, so I climbed in a window. I took her temperature. She has a fever, but it's slight. I thought it best to give her a bath and feed her before I brought her in. She took some water, but she won't eat. And her name is Winnifred. Winnie." I took a deep breath and finished: "She told me her name before she fell asleep in the car."

Hannah was staring at me with the oddest expression.

"What is it?" I asked, smoothing the child's hair.

"Nothing. I didn't expect to see you. Here, give her to me."

I transferred the child into her arms. I'd had no intention of ever returning to the Auditorium, of even driving near it. Until I'd climbed into my car, merely meaning to move it into the carriage house, and saw Kate's Red Cross bag lying up on the front seat. The list of addresses had fallen to the floor. We'd not had a chance to make our rounds yesterday before Hannah had called us in. Before Dr. Montee had spoken of a vaccine. Before my whole world had gone to pieces. And tempted as I was to throw the list into the fire and be done with it, I couldn't.

If not me, then who?

Hannah pressed the back of her hand against Winnie's cheek. "Where are her parents?" she asked.

"I don't know. She was alone. I searched the house and the yard. There was no one."

"Where does she live?"

"On Russell Street. Eight twenty-three Russell Street."

Hannah looked thoughtful. "A woman was brought in late last night. Someone found her wandering Morris in her nightgown. No shoes. No coat. He brought her here."

Morris was only a few blocks away from Russell.

"How is she?" I asked.

"I'll find out. Thank you, Cleo." Hannah adjusted the blanket around the girl and turned to go.

I stepped forward. "Hannah."

She turned.

"I wanted to say goodbye. For now. My brother's coming home Friday and I'm not sure . . . that is . . ." I trailed off, feeling terrible. What a time to abandon ship. "The truth is, I'm not supposed to be anywhere near here. I'm sorry, Hannah."

To my surprise, Hannah smiled. "Cleo, look at this child. Why are you sorry?"

I looked at the ground. "There are other children."

"And you are one person." Her tone was firm. "You've been a godsend. Just like Kate was. But there's such a thing as tempting fate." She leaned over and kissed my cheek. "Go. Keep your family close. I'll see you when this is all over with."

With that, Hannah left, Winnie cradled in her arms.

I left the Auditorium, my steps slow and tentative on the slick granite. I'd tried to find Edmund, but Sergeant LaBouef said he'd gone to Chinatown with some of the other soldiers. Patients had been turning up from the Chinese district, an area just south of the train station. Most of the men who lived there didn't have families, so no one thought to check on them. Edmund had gone to help. He wouldn't be back anytime soon.

The wind whipped at my scarf, lifting it off my red coat and flinging it over my shoulder. It was a strange feeling, walking around without pamphlets and masks, without my armband. Without Kate. I held my hat in place with one hand as I crossed the street.

I drove away without a backward glance.

CHAPTER TWENTY-FOUR

Thursday, October 24, 1918

The Bennetts lived on the eastern edge of town in a cherry-colored farmhouse. A dairy barn, also red, with a Gothic roof and adjacent silo, stood off to one side. Cows grazed in the yard, and the smell of hay and manure scented the air. I stood on the porch with my hand raised to knock. A voice drifted through an open window. Old and frail. An elderly man. I dropped my hand and listened.

"I have scheduled the service for Saturday, Mrs. Bennett. I'm afraid it will have to be very small, under the circumstances."

"I understand, Reverend Fitch. Thank you. There will just be my husband and myself. And the children, of course." Kate's mother sounded fragile and exhausted. And broken.

I lowered my head. What was I thinking, coming here? The Bennetts were in mourning. I was a stranger. I had not thought . . .

I'd lain in bed last night until a welcome exhaustion overtook me and I fell asleep. Then I had woken, dressed, and come here. No, I had not thought.

"Where is your husband, Mrs. Bennett?" Reverend Fitch asked. "I had hoped to discuss Katherine's arrangements with you both."

"John is upstairs. Resting. Katherine is . . . was his favorite, you see. I'm afraid he cannot bring himself to discuss her burial just yet."

"And your other children?"

"Waverley has gone back to St. Vincent's. Ruby and Etta have taken the younger children to my sister's."

There was a pause. "I see. Very well, I will place the funeral notice in the papers. That is no trouble at all. But I'm afraid we . . . we won't be able to have Katherine buried until the middle of November. Perhaps later."

I heard a gasp and my hand flew to cover my mouth, before I realized the sound had not come from me.

"The middle of November!" cried Mrs. Bennett. "That is weeks away!"

There was a long sigh. "I am sorry. Most of the men we hired to dig the graves are gone. Some have fallen ill themselves. Some have fled. I cannot find anyone who will take the job. The men we do have are working as fast as they can, I promise you."

"Couldn't we hire someone ourselves? We'll pay anything!"

"There is no one to hire. I am sorry, Cecily. More sorry than I can say. I have known that child since she was a baby. And if there was any strength left in these old bones, I would dig her grave myself. We have no choice but to wait."

I heard weeping. Through my own tears, I noticed the crepe on the door. Horrible, white, flickering in the wind. Careful, so as not to alert the house's occupants, I backed away. Down the steps, across the pathway, and through the gate, latching it carefully behind me.

No! What are you asking, missy? Lord have mercy!"

The caretaker looked scandalized. He eyed my worn overalls, the ones I used to help in the garden and never, ever wore in public. Until today. I could tell from his expression he was wondering if I was gassed. But I wasn't gassed. I was as sober and determined as the president of the Temperance Society.

"Mr. Tucker, I understand this is an . . . an unorthodox request," I said, using Jack's favorite term for all things preposterous. I gestured toward the caskets piled high against the cottage wall. The small stone house was situated in a far-off corner of the cemetery and served as the caretaker's home. "But you have dozens of people waiting to be buried. You're short on men. I can help."

Mr. Tucker spat, nearly spraying the caskets with thick, dark liquid. My stomach lurched. I struggled to keep my expression neutral. I did not want to do anything to offend this crusty old man. I needed his permission.

Mr. Tucker scratched his ear. "This Katherine Bennett. She's kin?"

"No, sir. She was a friend."

"Hasn't she got any brothers?"

"There are brothers, plenty of them. But the oldest two are in France. The rest are still little boys."

"In France, huh? My boy's off in Frogtown too. Fighting those good-for-nothing Krauts."

He chewed his cud, deliberating. He wavered. I could see it. I kept silent, looking across the graveyard to where a pretty stone church stood at the top of a small slope. Though regular gatherings were prohibited, brief funeral services were still allowed. All around us, the trees sheltered the gravestones, and the grass lay damp and matted from last night's storm. Men with shovels bent over muddy pits. There were three of them. Not nearly enough. The early-afternoon sun hid behind the clouds. I knew even that paltry light would disappear before long. I wished Mr. Tucker would hurry up and say yes. I did not want to be anywhere near this cemetery come nightfall.

Mr. Tucker shook his head. "No, I'm sorry. I sure could use the help, but I can't abide by a girl digging alone. It simply ain't done."

I opened my mouth to argue. From the other side of the cottage, I heard a car approach. The engine was cut, a door slammed. Then another. I closed my eyes, relief and fatigue threatening to send me to my knees. I wasn't sure if he'd come.

I should have known better.

I had stopped by the Auditorium after leaving the Bennetts'. Edmund hadn't been there, but I'd left word with Sergeant LaBouef, telling him where I'd be and why. The sergeant promised to deliver the message as soon as Edmund returned. Then I'd gone home to change and fetch a shovel. He must have raced over as soon as he heard.

I opened my eyes. "But I wouldn't be alone, Mr. Tucker. I wouldn't think of it. I'm sorry I was unclear."

"Then who . . ."

Edmund and Sergeant LaBouef rounded the side of the cottage. Both men were in uniform. They looked ready to march in a parade. Or a funeral procession. But instead of rifles, they gripped long-handled shovels. Edmund was white-faced. I could tell it cost him to stand there and not say a word.

I turned to Mr. Tucker. "I've brought help. You see? I've brought the army."

Mr. Tucker showed us to a far corner of the cemetery, where Kate's family had been laid to rest for generations. He dragged a shovel across the grass, marking the area to be dug. And then he walked off to send a message to Reverend Fitch, letting him know that the Bennetts could bury their daughter as early as tomorrow.

After that, the time passed in a blur. I dug until there were blisters on my hands and mud in my hair. I dripped with sweat. The sergeant insisted that I rest, that he and Edmund could finish without me. I snapped at him, this giant of a man, and he threw his hands up in defeat.

We dug. Off to one side, a mound of dirt grew larger and larger. Edmund forced his thermos into my hands and ordered me to drink. I drank. I focused on the dirt and the shovel and tried not to think of what I was doing.

As we finished, the sun descended into the horizon. I was so weary, my legs trembled. We stood at the edge of the open grave. Edmund held my hand tightly, and we bowed our heads. I sent a quiet message from my heart: *I wish I could have known you longer, Kate. Goodbye, my friend. God be with you till we meet again.* Aloud, I recited a psalm. The only one I could remember. "The Lord is my Shepherd; I shall not want . . ."

CHAPTER TWENTY-FIVE

Friday, October 25, 1918

One by one, the caskets left the train. The boxes were made of rough, unfinished pine, the work of a coffin maker far more concerned with volume than quality. One. Two. Three. Four. Five. Six.

Four men arranged the caskets along the platform in a single row. Dressed in stark black uniforms, their eyes were solemn above their white masks, their movements quiet and efficient. These were not the first bodies entrusted to their care.

Union Station teemed with people. Travelers and porters crowded the platform, wrapped in warm coats and hats to combat the fall chill. Red Cross canteen volunteers stood off to one side, distributing food and sundries to soldiers far from home. There were people like me, who waited, impatient, for loved ones to make their way back to the city.

But for a moment no one spoke. Men removed their hats and lowered their heads. Women pressed gloved hands to their lips. The only sound came from the train's powerful engine and the distant whistle of a departed express. And all around me, people thought the same awful, guilty words.

There but for the grace of God go I.

I looked across the tracks and up to where a clock tower rose high above the station. Ten minutes past seven.

Twenty more minutes.

The vigil ended. Something thumped against my leg. I looked down. A boy of five or six scampered by, tugged along by his distracted mother. He clutched a toy ship in one hand, the wood painted red, white, and blue. They boarded a train.

Determined not to stare holes into the clock, I turned back to the Red Cross booth. Cheerful women dispensed sandwiches, coffee, Juicy Fruit, and Lucky Strikes in vast quantities. A trio of navy recruits gathered around a slim, curly-haired blonde, the prettiest of the group.

I wore a coat the color of caramel, my last clean one, and gripped a long black umbrella before me like a cane. My fingers, wrapped in brown leather, drummed against the curved wooden handle. I forced myself to stop and did my best to ignore the dull throbbing behind my eyeballs. A persistent headache, an unwanted companion since morning. I looked at the clock again.

Nineteen more minutes.

A wail, high-pitched and sudden, made me jump. I exchanged a startled look with the soldier beside me. Leaning forward, I glanced past him. A small group of men and women had converged on the caskets. An older woman had flung herself across one of them, her shoulders shaking with the force of her weeping. A gray-haired man tried to coax her away, his own face twisted in anguish.

I looked down at my shoes, unable to watch. The soldier did the same.

Minutes later, all but one of the caskets had been collected and whisked away to waiting trucks. Two uniformed men stood beside the last body, scanning the area for a final claimant. The others would be en route to the city's mortuaries, I knew, and I wondered how long it would be before they were finally laid to rest.

The train stood ready to leave. Wheels churned and smoke billowed forth, enveloping the night sky. The engine was loud enough to sting the eardrums. From the platform, I felt the vibrations beneath my feet. Porters rushed to remove the small steps positioned by the train doors. A bearded conductor cupped both hands to his mouth and hollered, "All aboard! This is the number fifty-three for Seattle, Victoria, and all points north! Have your tickets ready, please!" He swung onto the train with a grace that belied his considerable girth. After one last call, the train chugged out of sight.

Another whistle blasted almost immediately. And as the glossy black passenger train pulled in, I heard, "Union Station, Portland! All depart for Union Station, Portland!"

Anticipation surged within me, as did an overwhelming sense of relief. This was the Southern Pacific number thirteen.

At last.

Passengers spilled from the train, crowding the platform in a sea of humanity. Most were masked. A few were not, including me. Craning my neck, I tried to catch a glimpse of Jack and Lucy. But bit by bit, the crowd dispersed, leaving only a few travelers in the area.

Reaching into my coat pocket, I pulled out Jack's telegram. I reread it, then looked at the number on the side of the train. This was the correct train. This was the correct day. Where were they?

I hastened toward the passageway and across the tracks. Barely keeping my frustration in check as the old woman before me shuffled forth at the speed of molasses. Finally, I pushed through the glass doors and walked into the station's large, high-ceilinged lobby. It was overheated. I felt the oppressive warmth wrap itself around me like a wool blanket in August. Ignoring the discomfort, I searched, and dismissed, one unfamiliar face after another.

My insides congealed into something cold and unpleasant. My

headache intensified. I stood in the center of the elegant marble-floored lobby. I turned, one final, slow circle, before the truth sank deep within me like a stone.

They had not come. They were not here. What could have happened?

A barrel-chested porter studied his pocket watch by the doors. I hurried over.

"Excuse me, but is this the train from Klamath Falls?" I pointed toward the tracks.

The porter looked at me beneath thick black brows. "It is, miss." His gravelly voice was muffled by his mask. "The Southern Pacific number thirteen. That is correct."

"I don't understand. My brother and sister-in-law were supposed to be on this train. They sent word." I held up my crumpled telegram.

The porter studied it. "It's possible there was some delay, and they simply missed their train. Do you have a telephone number? Or an address?"

I felt foolish for not thinking of it. "Yes, of course."

"Well, come along. You can use the telephone in the office. If it's still working, that is." He offered his arm. I took it. There had to be an explanation. Perhaps Lucy was feeling poorly. Didn't pregnant women tire easily? Especially early on? Jack must have decided to delay their trip so she could rest. There would be another telegram waiting for me when I returned home. That was it. I'd started to panic for nothing.

The ticket seller gave us a distracted glance. A thin man with black hair slicked with brilliantine, he stood behind a high counter. I took care not to brush my skirt against the cuspidors positioned by the wooden benches. Several of the brass containers oozed a nasty grayish spittle, the result of several failed aims.

A closed door was to the right of the counter. A sign above it read PRIVATE. The attendant patted my arm before releasing it. He pulled an oversize ring from his belt, squinting at the assortment of keys. "Let's see, which of these . . . Aha!" Shaking one free, he inserted it into the lock.

We walked into a small office. What looked like several decades' worth of company ledgers teetered in untidy piles on the desk, nearly swallowing the telephone that stood in its midst.

The porter gestured toward the telephone. "There you are, miss."

"Thank you, Mr. . . . ." I offered my hand.

He took it. "Latham. Alfred Latham."

"Mr. Latham. Thank you, sir."

Mr. Latham waved away my thanks. "Take all the time you need. I'm sure there's a simple explanation." He left, closing the door behind him.

Leaning my umbrella against the desk, I lifted the receiver. I hoped the telephone operator today would be merciful and agree to connect me. She was. I gave her the information and breathed a sigh of relief when I heard a male voice, brisk and pleasant, on the other end.

"The Baldwin Hotel. Good evening. This is Maxwell Bauer."

"Good evening, Mr. Bauer. I'm calling for Jackson Berry."

"I'm very sorry, miss, but the Berrys departed earlier today."

The words, so cheerfully relayed, felt like a slap.

"Are you certain?" I asked, fighting to remain calm. "My name is Cleo Berry. Jackson is my brother. Jack and Luciane were scheduled to arrive here in Portland this evening, but they weren't on the train. Can you help me?"

There was a silence. When Mr. Bauer spoke, I heard his concern. "Miss Berry, your brother and Mrs. Berry were escorted to the train station by Mr. Wilson, our driver. If you will please hold, I'll speak to him myself."

"I will hold. Thank you."

"I'll be just a moment."

My fingers drummed against the desk, a nervous, uneven tempo. It felt like ages before Mr. Bauer returned.

"Miss Berry, I'm sorry. Mr. Wilson was very clear. He drove the Berrys to the station and loaded their trunks onto the . . ." Paper crinkled in the background. "Onto the Southern Pacific northbound, number thirteen." He paused again. "He watched them board the train. And he saw it leave the station."

I braced a palm against the desk, dizzy. "I see." My voice registered just above a whisper. "Thank you."

"I'm sorry I could not be of more help. I would like to add that I saw the Berrys this morning before they departed. They looked to be in perfect health. I'm certain it's not what you think. There must be a simple explanation."

A simple explanation. Why did everyone keep insisting on that?

"Yes, I'm sure of it also. Good evening, Mr. Bauer."

"Good evening, Miss Berry. And good luck."

I went back to the waiting room and studied the schedule above the ticket counter. There was another train arriving from the south, an incoming Shasta Express scheduled for 9:05 p.m. I looked at the clock above the departure doors. It was nearly eight o'clock.

The coffin keepers shuffled past, carrying their unclaimed charge toward the front doors. The kind Mr. Latham was nowhere to be seen. Tossing my umbrella onto an empty bench, I dropped beside it and waited.

I leaped to my feet with the arrival of the Shasta Express. Jack and Lucy were not on that train, but there was one more coming in. At 11:20 p.m. Surely they would be on that one.

My eyes were pinned to the clock. The ticket seller walked by, his shift ended for the night. His attention was fixed firmly on his shoes, as if he sensed my terror and was afraid it was contagious. Contagious. Ha! I bit back a laugh, the edges stitched with hysteria. I knew what he thought and hated him for it.

There but for the grace of God go I.

The lobby was no longer warm. I pulled my coat closer, wondering if the heating had been shut off.

At eleven o'clock, I walked out onto the platform. The crowd had thinned. The canteen was closed. I unfolded my timetable so I could view the Southern Pacific route in its entirety.

The number thirteen train had originated from San Francisco's Market Street station. I scrolled down two-thirds of the way until I found Klamath Falls nestled between Midland and Chiloquin. Jack and Lucy's train had left Klamath Falls at a quarter past nine this morning. How many stops were there between Klamath Falls and Portland? Ashland, Tolo, Gold Hill, Grants Pass, Wolf Creek . . . the list marched on. I felt my heart sink.

Please. Please let them be on this train.

A whistle sounded. I started to fold the timetable. Stopped when I saw a drop of blood on the white paper. I reached up, touched my nose, and saw red on my knuckle. Even as I drew out a handkerchief and pressed it to my face, a strange awareness settled within me. Fear, but also resignation. A sense that this moment had always been inevitable. After everything that had happened, how could I have dared to imagine anything different? My family. Edmund. A future.

The train pulled in. Passengers disembarked, calling out and jostling. I looked around and wondered where Kate was. I stumbled. A hand reached out to steady me. I looked up, up.

And there was my brother.

Jack stared at me, gray eyes wide with shock and horror. He took in my soaked handkerchief, pressed a hand against my cheek. "Cleo," he said. "Jesus Christ!"

I heard a cry behind him. Lucy. From far away, I heard Jack say, *She's bleeding. She's on fire. Get help!* Lucy's hands, cool and soft, were on my face. She was crying. I wanted to tell her I was fine. That it did not hurt.

But before I could, I saw over her shoulder a small boy sitting on my old swing. I wondered how it was possible to see him. Were we at home? But he was there, with his mop of hair, black as pitch, and eyes the color of whiskey. Lucy's eyes. The boy was giggling and shrieking and crying, *Higher, higher!* Jack stood behind him. My brother was smiling, but there was a tightness around his mouth and sorrow in his eyes. I knew he was remembering another child. The sister he'd once pushed on that very swing. I was sad I would not have the chance to know this little boy.

I would have been the greatest aunt ever.

They vanished. I saw Edmund. He was different. Older. He sat by a fireplace with a book in his hand. A woman leaned over and kissed him. He smiled at her. The woman was brown-haired and blue-eyed and pretty. She was not me. I felt a twinge of regret.

Had life been different, had there been more time . . . I could have loved Edmund Parrish desperately.

My brother was lifting me up, up. He was running. My head fell back, and I saw the night sky, filled with a million twinkling diamonds. Ah, well. It would be nice to hold my mama again. And my father. And to laugh with Kate. So be it.

It was a fine night to die.

CHAPTER TWENTY-SIX

Tuesday, November 12, 1918

When I woke, the war had ended. I did not know it at the time. My world had grown small. A room, a bed, a body that felt as though it belonged to someone else entirely. Someone old and weak, with one foot toeing the grave.

I opened my eyes.

Jack was sitting in my bedside chair, watching me. He had a beard—an odd sight. Lucy didn't like beards. He held my sketchbook in his hands.

"You open your eyes sometimes," he said quietly. "And you close them. And I'm not sure if you understand anything I've said. Can you hear me, Cleo?" He waited, and when I didn't respond, he said, "Hannah Flynn's been by. I wish you'd wake up, so I could yell at you good and proper." He dropped his head onto the bedding, by my arm. "But when I think of you, just a kid, waiting in that carriage, I understand why you did it."

"Lucy."

Jack's head snapped up. He searched my face, and I felt his hands, large and warm, wrap around one of mine. "Cleo?"

"Lucy?" I asked again, not recognizing my own voice. It was dry and whispery, a ghost.

"She's fine, darlin'. The baby too. She's sleeping. It's three in the morning."

Lucy was safe. I felt myself sinking, wanting to rest. I struggled to stay awake. "Edmund?"

My brother looked mystified. I realized he didn't know who Edmund was. He didn't recognize his name. Edmund hadn't been by, and that could only mean one thing.

"Parrish," I said, forcing myself to finish. When had it happened? I had to know.

"I know who he is, Cleo." Jack looked past me. "Turn your head. He's right here."

I turned, slowly, my head throbbing the entire while. The pain was worth it. Before I fell back into darkness, I saw Edmund on my window seat, fast asleep against a pile of pillows. Looking just as I remembered. And beyond him, through the glass, was the largest moon I'd ever seen.

CHAPTER TWENTY-SEVEN

Thursday, January 16, 1919

Through the window, I could see Lucy making her way toward the school doors. Jack was in Victoria until tomorrow, on business, and Lucy and I were to spend the rest of the afternoon at the shops. As she was wrapped in a long black coat with a fur collar, one could not tell she was in a family way. But even from this distance, I could see how healthy she looked. Despite Lucy's history and the influenza, despite everything, the baby would come in July. My niece or nephew. I could not wait.

Miss Abernathy's voice interrupted my thoughts. "... on thinking before one speaks. Can anyone recall President Lincoln's exact words? Anyone? Hmm? Miss Berry?"

I turned my head. "'It is better to remain silent and be thought a fool,'" I said, "'than to open one's mouth and remove all doubt.'"

"That is close enough. Thank you. Now, who can tell me why . . ."

I looked out the window again. Nearly three months ago, a suspicious train conductor, thinking Lucy looked sickly, had demanded she and Jack disembark at the next stop. My brother refused, explaining she was only tired from the baby. *My wife is well. We have paid for this car. We will remain on board.* But the conductor would not be swayed. When the train pulled into Yoncalla, Jack, Lucy, and five other passengers were forced off. They'd had to wait hours for the next train. And when they'd finally arrived, weary and aggravated, at Union Station, I'd collapsed at their feet.

It had been a bad time for everyone.

Beside me, Grace propped her book up on the desk so Miss Abernathy wouldn't see the letter she wrote to Anthony, a boy she'd met in Florence during the epidemic. There was a funny, dopey look on her face, the kind Margaret used to have whenever she spoke of Harris.

Margaret was gone, her chair in the back of the classroom empty. She'd run away with Harris the day school closed, so that he would not have to report for training at Fort Stevens. She'd sent her parents two postcards from Canada. One from Vancouver. One from Toronto. And then, just after Thanksgiving, a telegram had arrived — both Margaret and Harris had died in Quebec, of influenza.

Three other schoolmates had passed on. Emily had recovered,

though her lungs remained weak. Her father had arrived from Hawaii to bring her home. Thinking of them all, I wanted to weep. But I felt like a dishrag that had been wrung out to dry. There were no more tears left in me.

We had a new housekeeper. Mrs. Dinwiddie was lovely and cheery and made delicious fried chicken. But it wasn't the same. I missed Mrs. Foster. She'd recovered from the influenza. Her son and grandchildren had too. But her daughter-in-law had not, and Mrs. Foster had chosen to remain in Hood River, to be close to her family.

And Edmund. He would be gone too. His train would leave on Saturday for New York, where he would finish his studies at the Rockefeller Institute for Medical Research. He wanted to be a bacteriologist: an expert in infectious diseases. At the Rockefeller Institute, he'd learn from some of the best scientists in the world. A fearsome group of men and women, with all sorts of awards and letters printed after their names. I was happy for him. I was. This was an important opportunity. I told myself that it was enough to know that he was out there somewhere, and that he was safe. Though it was hard. He was still here, in this city, and already I missed him.

I felt strange sometimes, restless. Being in this classroom, in this town—where everything *looked* normal. The masks were gone, the shops open, the ribbons pulled from the doors. People smiled and laughed and visited. But no one spoke of what had happened. Lucy said it had been too much. That people needed to forget the war and influenza both.

The bell rang. Chairs scraped as we gathered our books.

"Cleo." Louisa stood by my desk, holding out a small book. "I found this in your old room, under the bed. May I borrow it?"

I started to ask what she was doing rifling around under my old bed and then decided I didn't want to know. Taking the book from her, I glanced at the title. *Famous American Women: Vignettes from the Past and Present.* I hadn't realized it was missing. I thought about how I'd felt last fall—anxious about my future, worried because my entire life had not been neatly mapped out before me. I still didn't know who I wanted to be, what I wanted to study, not for sure. But the uncertainty felt like a small thing now; it no longer bothered me.

I handed the book back to Louisa. "You may keep it," I said.

She looked surprised, then suspicious. "You're letting me have it?"

I nodded. "I don't need it anymore." Smiling, Louisa thanked me and walked off.

Grace turned to me. "Fanny and I are going to the pictures Saturday night. The new Mary Pickford movie is out. I know Edmund is leaving in the morning. But will you come after?"

I could tell she expected me to refuse. I'd been saying no a lot, preferring Edmund's company, or solitude. I wanted to refuse, but Grace looked worried and sad. Margaret had been her friend too.

And out of nowhere, I remembered a conversation that took place a lifetime ago. *I was stabbed five times, Cleo. I keep thinking I never should have made it home from France. At the very least, I shouldn't be able to use this hand. I figure every day I've had since then is a windfall.*

Like Edmund, I'd been given a second chance to live my life.

A reprieve.

A windfall.

Margaret and Kate were gone. But Grace, she was right here. And I thought it would be nice for once to sit in a dark theater, to watch the new Mary Pickford movie and not think so much. Maybe if I tried harder, I could feel like my old self again. At least a little bit.

And so I smiled. And I said, "Thank you, yes, I'd love to come."

CHAPTER TWENTY-EIGHT

Friday, January 17, 1919

We had only meant to go on a drive. A quick trip across the bridge, perhaps, because there was no such thing as privacy at home with my brother around. Instead, Edmund and I had found ourselves here, stopped on Third Street, looking up at a building that held too many memories for both of us. Mostly bad ones.

"Even the outside looks different." I peered out the car window. It was late afternoon, after school. The air was cold and damp. The only other person about was a man with a cane, walking his dog.

"It's quiet," Edmund said from the driver's seat. His face had filled out some, and the shadows were gone from his green eyes. "The ambulances are gone. And the families on the steps."

He was right. I'd grown so accustomed to the noise — the

sirens, the men, women, and children weeping—that this calmness struck me as odd.

The worst of the Spanish influenza had passed through the city by Thanksgiving, enough so that the health office had closed down the Auditorium's emergency services. A fumigation crew had been called in. The building would reopen to the public for the first time next week. It felt wrong to me, seeing the advertisements in the newspaper. The symphony would be playing next Friday, and the following week, three evening performances of *Hamlet* were scheduled, plus a matinee on Sunday.

"Do you want to go in?" Edmund asked.

I turned to him, surprised. "Will they let us?"

"I'm sure I could talk our way in if you wanted. Hannah stopped by last week. She said the chairs are all back in place. The red ones. And the carpets." He paused. "The piano that was in the basement . . . it's been put back onstage."

Hearing this last part made my throat tighten. "It looks like it did before," I said. "As if nothing happened."

Edmund reached for my hand, pressed a kiss against it. "You don't have to," he said quietly. "I'm not sure I'm ready to see it either."

I looked at the Auditorium. I thought of the musicians and actors who would come back. Life was slowly returning to something that looked normal. But what about me? Would I ever be able to think of this building as anything other than a hospital? To walk onto the orchestra floor, all dressed up, and not see the men and women and children on their cots? Or the floors slick with blood and worse? Or the soldiers on the stage? Would I be able to sit in one of those chairs, program in hand, and not think of Kate?

I looked down at Edmund's hand in mine. Seconds passed. I shook my head. Edmund gave my hand one last squeeze, and a moment later we were driving away. I forced myself not to look back, concentrating on the buildings that flew past, and the man walking his dog, and the raindrops that began to fall from the sky.

Maybe one day I'll go back, I thought. *Someday.*

But not yet.

HISTORICAL NOTE

Although the characters in this story are fictional, the events that took place are not. Between 1918 and 1920, an estimated 30 million to 50 million people worldwide died from Spanish influenza—more than died in World War I; more than were killed by the Black Death of the fourteenth century. Nearly 675,000 Americans were among the dead. Though the pandemic's origins have never been confirmed, most experts agree it did not come from Spain. Strong evidence suggests a strain of the influenza virus may have originated in Haskell County, Kansas, early in 1918. From there, it likely spread to a nearby military base before moving on to Europe and the rest of the world.

What is particularly chilling about Spanish flu is that it struck not only children and the elderly, as is typical, but healthy young men and women. So great was the number of dead among soldiers, nurses, students, and pregnant women that one doctor noted, "They were doubly dead in that they died so young."

The first outbreak of flu in the Pacific Northwest came in late September 1918, when a trainload of troops from the Boston area arrived at Camp Lewis in Washington State. Illness spread rapidly throughout the region. On October 11, 1918, the Portland mayor George L. Baker ordered all mass activities shut down, including schools, club meetings, theaters, church services, and parades. His decision was echoed in towns and cities across the United States as health officials tried to forestall an epidemic by preventing large groups from congregating.

Despite their efforts, the death toll was high. The Oregon State Board of Health reported 48,146 cases of Spanish influenza, with a mortality rate of 3,675 for the period of October 1, 1918, to September 30, 1920. A third of those deaths were in Portland. Mortality counts across the country were grim: Salt Lake City, 576; Omaha, nearly 1,200; Seattle, over 1,400; Minneapolis, nearly 2,000; Washington, D.C., 2,895; San Francisco, over 3,000; Boston, 4,794 in the fall of 1918 alone; Philadelphia, 12,191; New York City, 20,608.

Portland's Public Auditorium, only a year old at the time, was one of several emergency hospitals established. It was managed by the city and the American Red Cross, and eventually by the U.S. Army's Spruce Division. Decades later the building was remodeled and renamed the Keller Auditorium. Very little of the original structure remains.

The American Red Cross was founded by Clara Barton in 1881. In its early years, the humanitarian organization provided disaster relief during the Johnstown Flood of 1889, the Spanish-American War, and the San Francisco Earthquake of 1906. But it was during World War I that the Red Cross experienced tremendous growth. Prior to the war, there were 107 chapters throughout the country. By 1918 the number had jumped to 3,864. Participation was considered a patriotic duty for the war effort. Schoolchildren collected fruit pits; the carbon from the pits was used to make gas masks. Additionally, women produced great quantities of sweaters, socks, blankets, and medical supplies for soldiers at home and abroad.

During the Spanish influenza outbreak, there were tales of people who were too scared to care for neighbors, and of men and women who abandoned their homes and families out of fear. But there were many other stories as well—of ordinary people who traveled door-to-door in search of strangers who might be ill, who helped in hospitals, who delivered food, who cared for orphans. Many worked tirelessly until the moment they were stricken with influenza themselves. Their quiet acts of heroism served as inspiration for Cleo's story.

FOR FURTHER READING

Barry, John. *The Great Influenza: The Epic Story of the Deadliest Plague in History*. New York: Viking, 2004.

Blanke, David. *The 1910s*. Westport, Conn.: Greenwood, 2002.

Crosby, Alfred W. *America's Forgotten Pandemic: The Influenza of 1918*. New York: Cambridge University Press, 1989.

Maxwell, William. *They Came Like Swallows*. New York: Modern Library, 1997.

Nelson, Donald R. *Historic Photos of Portland*. Nashville, Tenn.: Turner Publishing, 2006.

ACKNOWLEDGMENTS

I would like to express my deepest gratitude to Suzie Townsend. She is part agent, part fairy godmother, and I am lucky to have her in my corner. My editor, Adah Nuchi, is wise and kind, a pleasure to work with. I am indebted to her and to the entire team at Houghton Mifflin Harcourt Books for Young Readers.

A special thanks to Jennifer Soulagnet for bravely reading the original draft. The talented Jenny Bowles not only took my author photos, but treated me to one adventure-filled morning in Potlatch, Idaho. Kathryn Santos, archivist for the California State Railroad Museum Library, discovered an old Southern Pacific timetable and sent it my way. Maija Anderson, head of Historical Collections and Archives for Oregon Health and Science University, graciously answered a stranger's query regarding early-twentieth-century medical school requirements. I am also obliged to the staff of the Oregon Historical Society, who helped me locate one document key to Cleo's story—an old diagram of the Public Auditorium.

And, lastly, I would like to say thank you to my family, for everything. Thank you to Melissa Preciado; to my husband, Chris; and to Mia Evangeline, my sweet girl, for keeping those pencils nice and sharp.